A Kate Robbins Teen Psychic Suspense

Book One

By award-winning author of SCARS, HUNTED, and STAINED

Cheryl Rainfield

Visions was previously published as Parallel Visions; I rewrote it to have queer main characters and be full length, the way I wanted it.

C. Rainfield

Published by C. Rainfield
www.CherylRainfield.com

This is a work of fiction. All characters, places, and events described are imaginary. Any resemblance to real people, places, and events is entirely coincidental.

Cataloging Publication Data

Rainfield, C. (Cheryl)

Visions: A Teen Psychic Novel / by Cheryl Rainfield

Summary: Queer teen Kate sees psychic visions, but only when she's having an asthma attack. When she "sees" her sister being beaten, she needs more visions to save her, along with her crush's suicidal sister—but triggering her asthma could kill her. Can the two teens work together to save their sisters?

ISBN: 978-0-9878460-3-7 (Paperback)

[1. Domestic Abuse—Fiction. 2. Rape—Fiction 3. Suicidal Ideation—Fiction. 5. Lesbians—Fiction. 6. Nonbinary—Fiction. 7. Asthma—Fiction. 8. Clairvoyance--Fiction] 1. Title

Previously published as Parallel Visions; this edition has been extensively rewritten to be full length with queer main characters.

Cover design by Mousam Banerjee

Printed by KDP Publishing in the United States of America

Your Free eBook Is Waiting

Kendra's father's trial is only three months away, and she's dreading it. Her mother has become critical, and keeps fighting with Kendra's girlfriend Meghan.

Kendra hasn't cut in months, but everything is starting to feel too hard. Will she be able to keep from cutting?

Grab a copy FADED SCARS, a 38-page SCARS short story
https://www.cherylrainfield.com/newsletter/

Author's Note

THIS NOVEL HAS STRONG queer and nonbinary teen characters with paranormal powers who fight to save others, heal, and love. They also face or talk about various forms of trauma—domestic abuse, rape, queerphobia, and bullying—the way many teens do today, and the way I did myself; our society is white supremist, misogynist, ableist, and queerphobic. But I believe there is hope and strength in our healing and working together, the way my characters do.

My books are my voice, and my way to encourage healing. I believe when we talk about trauma and abuse, and our healing from it, it can help others heal and find their voices, and encourage greater empathy for both themselves and for others. I'm a nonbinary lesbian and a rape and cult torture survivor who's had asthma (though not as badly as the main character). I've drawn on some of these experiences as well as my healing, inner strength, and hope for a better world. If you need to put the book down, you can always come back to it when you're ready. If you need support, please check out the resources at the end of this book; there are more on my website CherylRainfield.com.

I hope you feel seen in this book, and that you see your own strength and healing. Take good, gentle care of yourself.

Content Note

Please be aware: This book contains content that some people may find triggering, including: partner abuse; mention of rape and death; attempted murder; attempted suicide; queerphobia; cyber bullying; and asthma.

Dedication

FOR THE QUEER KIDS, the abused kids (and adults), for everyone who has faced oppression and bigotry, survived trauma, and is working to find their voice or has already found it —I am glad you are here. It will get better, especially as you find community. I hope you believe in yourself and see your own strength. You belong here.

For the teachers, the librarians, the parent groups, the organizations like PENAmerica, and everyone else fighting book bans, working to protect every child's and teen's right to read the books that help them know they're not alone, and who give them a safe space—I appreciate you so much. You are needed.

And for Jean, who is like a mom to me, who always believes in me, and who loves fantasy and magic as much as I do.

My throat feels too narrow but I push past it, blowing so hard into my peak flow meter that the kitchen spins and undulates before my eyes. My glasses slide down my nose. *Please don't let me have another attack—or another vision of someone who won't believe the danger they're in.*

Mom's beside me before I can inhale, yanking the peak flow meter out of my hand.

I try to stifle the wheeze that wants to escape from my lungs.

"Hmm," Mom says. The meter is in the yellow zone, but closer to the green than the red. "How'd you sleep last night?"

I clear my throat. "Fine. And the readout is practically green. I'm ready to go back to school."

"Your health is more important than your desire to see your friends, Kate," Mom says, a snap in her voice.

What friends? I clear my throat. "My levels are good, I've got my quick relief inhaler—" I prime my puffer and inhale the medicine. "And I've taken my dose, and my regular meds, too. I haven't had a big attack—" or a vision "In days. It's time to let me go back."

Mom laughs. "Only you would want to go to school on a Monday."

I miss seeing Desi's kind, beautiful face. Miss hearing Ms. Hirano talk so excitedly about books. Miss the normalcy of school, of seeing other students my age, even if I am outside it all. I'm out so often most kids don't even know my name, or talk to me when I'm there. But Desi does.

I want so badly to feel like a normal teen, not somebody with severe asthma who's almost died. Not somebody who gets visions of the future every time I have an asthma attack, visions of people I can't protect.

Just thinking about them makes my lungs feel full of sharp rocks. Why do I get these visions if I can't help anyone? No one ever believes me—not my parents, my sister, or the professionals who are supposed to protect others. Not most of the people who were at risk themselves. And even when they did I couldn't protect them from the bad things I saw happening—no matter what I did.

I flash to Navaeh gasping for breath in her hospital bed next to mine, the nurse running in, the stricken look on her parents' faces. To Zoey getting kidnapped.

I clench my hands, my lips trembling. No; I'm not going there. Not going to get sucked into the despair again.

"All right," Mom says, gently. "You can go. If you make sure you use your inhaler if you need it, tell a teacher if you have an attack, and call me."

"I will." It's the same thing every time.

Mom looks at me sternly. "No pushing yourself to be like the other kids. You're not."

No, I'm not, in more ways than one: Being chronically ill. Being lesbian in a world that pushes heteronormativity so hard. Having visions of people I can't protect.

My first vision came when I almost died from an asthma attack when I was three. Now I get visions every time I struggle to breathe—little fragments of what could happen, or what already has. It's like being deprived of air woke up something in my brain, something that everyone has but doesn't listen to. Or that's what I tell myself so I feel less like a freak.

"I know," I say.

"I know you do." Mom sighs. "I just want you to be more careful with your health. Take it more seriously." She rubs her eyes, her fingers bumping against her glasses. "I want you to catch your symptoms sooner, stop ignoring them just to fit in with the cool kids."

"I'm not—" But it doesn't matter what I say; she'll never believe me. Not when I've tried to hide my symptoms too many times and then paid for it. "I'll be more careful." I pick up my backpack, sling it over one shoulder. "See you later." I kiss her cheek, then stride out the door before she can change her mind.

Outside, the heavy May air is hot and humid, carrying pollen and air pollution—something most people don't even notice. It clogs my chest like oatmeal, tightening my throat.

I wonder if I've made a mistake. I take a quick puff from my inhaler and keep walking steadily, the sun warming my skin, the rush of cars on the street beside me like the background rhythm in a song.

I'm free again. The day's only got to get better—especially with Desi in it.

A goofy smile takes over my face, and I scowl to wipe it off. I know Desi's kind to everyone, especially the kids they think need it. They'll never see me the way I see them. Not me, the perpetual sick kid.

I march on, my steps robotic. I wish I could make them see me the way I see them. No, not even that. I wish I could make them see me as someone healthy, someone who doesn't need their compassion and protectiveness. Someone who's not sick.

FIRST PERIOD ENGLISH AND Desi is already here. They wiggle their fingers at me, their warm brown eyes and full lips smiling. My face grows hot. I slip into my seat, ducking my head.

Desi's gorgeous, with their smooth bronze skin, strong, supple body, their jeans tight, and their thick, dark hair half shaved. The silver rings on their fingers shine in the light, and they're always wearing queer T-shirts, out and proud as a nonbinary lesbian. But what draws me to them the most is how compassionate they are.

I've seen them translate for another Mexican kid, stop bullies from tormenting a girl and then comfort her, and give half their lunch to a student who didn't have any. They've never teased me about my asthma, and they're friendly with me when most other students look past me like I don't exist.

"Hey, mouth breather," Gabby hisses at me, leaning over in her seat to make sure I know she's talking to me. As if it isn't obvious.

I keep my gaze focused on Ms. Hirano, even as my face heats up. I should be used to it by now, but it hurts every time. I can't make myself not asthmatic; I would if I could.

"Hey wheeze bag!" Gabby says, a bit louder.

I stiffen, glancing at Desi, hoping they didn't hear. They're reading a book, leaning back casually with one arm over their chair, not bothered by anything. Ms. Hirano's writing on the whiteboard, her back to us.

My cell vibrates in my pocket. I slip it out.

Take your inhaler if you need to, Mom texts.

I will, I text back.

I wish she wouldn't worry so much. Wish I could complain to Jenna about it, but now she always takes Mom's side. It's like she became a mini-Mom with me, always checking on my health—to get Mom's approval.

When I was young Jenna used to make me laugh when I was in the hospital, sit on my bed and play cards with me, tell me stories about her teachers or the other kids. She'd introduce me to her friends during a video chat, or sneak me home chocolate or chips during Mom's super-clean eating phase she forced us all to do to see if it would help my asthma—and to force me to lose some weight.

But Jenna became jealous about all the time Mom spent with me because of my asthma. She stopped wanting to hang out with me, complaining that my being sick interfered with her life. It got worse when she started dating Mason—and then when she eloped.

The house still seems too empty without her. Dad doesn't know what to do with himself; he used to spend all his free time coaching Jenna in sports. He can't do that with me. And Mom just hovers over me.

I ram my cell back into my pocket. It feels like almost every conversation Mom and I have is about my asthma, like that's all there is between us.

Ms. Hirano turns around to face the class and claps her hands. "Book banning has been in the news a lot lately," she says, looking intently at us. Even in her pantsuit and high heels she looks different than most other teachers, with the streaks of color in her long black hair and her friendly, engaging manner. She's the only out trans teacher I've ever had and one of the reasons I want to come to school. "Can you tell me a title that's frequently been banned?"

My hand shoots up in the air, even though I usually try to keep a low profile.

Ms. Hirano's eyebrows rise. "Yes, Kate?"

I clear my throat. "*All Boys Aren't Blue, Last Night at the Telegraph Club, Melissa,* and *Scars.*"

Ms. Hirano writes the titles on the whiteboard. "And what do all those books have in common?"

"Queer characters," I say. "And queer authors, too."

Desi nods. "You said it."

Someone else snickers. Homophobe. I don't hide being queer with my rainbow glasses, bright rainbow backpack and the buttons I've pinned on it, and my rainbow shoelaces. It took me years to come out to my parents, and now I don't ever want to hide. There's something so freeing in being all of me. I want the kids who don't feel safe enough to come out yet to know they're not alone. And straight people to be reminded that we're here.

"Exactly," Ms. Hirano says.

"Miss, are you sure we should be talking about this?" Imani asks, without raising her hand. "Won't you get in trouble?"

Ms. Hirano runs her hand through her hair, the pink and blue highlights standing out.

"Those books should be banned," Gabby says, spittle flying from her mouth. "They're against everything in the bible."

"No, they're not," Desi says, leaning back in their chair like they're confident in what they say, and comfortable in their body. "The word homosexual wasn't even written into the bible until nineteen forty-six, and it was a mistranslation—probably a deliberate one."

I grin at them.

Gabby sputters. "That's—that's a lie!"

"No, the misinterpretations in the bible are a lie," Desi says.

I laugh, then clap my hand over my mouth.

Ms. Hirano holds up her hands. "While that's very relevant information, I'd like to get the conversation back to book banning," she says. "And yes, Imani, this is something we absolutely should be talking about in a class that discusses books."

"But—"

Ms. Hirano keeps talking. "Have any of you read the books Kate mentioned? Or any others that were recently banned?"

"I loved all the ones Kate mentioned," Desi calls out. "And I'd add *Juliet Takes A Breath, Cemetery Boys, Felix Ever After,* and *Gender Queer.*"

My cheeks burn hotter. They noticed me again! And they love some of the same books as I do. I need to read the rest.

"Yeah, how about banned books by Black, brown, and Indigenous authors?" Zoey says, bobbing her head, her gorgeous locs bouncing. "I've read *The Hate U Give, Monday's Not Coming, Stamped,* and *The Absolutely True Diary of A Part Time Indian,* just to name a few. They're being banned big time, too."

Ms. Hirano writes them on the whiteboard. "And why do you think that is?" She points her marker at the class.

"Because far-right Christians are racist, transphobic, and homophobic," Desi says, then turns and grins at me, winking.

I'm so shocked I can't even smile at them. Desi turns back around.

"You said it!" Zoey calls.

Gabby leaps up from her seat. "You're all being prejudiced against Christians!" she says.

"Aw, shut it," Jahome says lazily.

"Jahome, what have I said about personal attacks?" Ms. Hirano perches on the edge of her desk. "Our classroom can have lively discussions, but no denigrating others."

"But Desi was picking on me, too!" Gabby says.

"No, I was just stating facts about transphobic, racist Christians. Is that you?" Desi asks.

Gabby splutters again. I love that Desi can make her speechless.

"Again, what do all those banned books have in common?" Ms. Hirano asks.

"That they're by Black and brown or queer authors!" Jahome says, waving his hand wildly. "Or about characters who are."

"But it's not just marginalized authors or books," Desi says, leaning forward. "They're banning books about mental health and sexual violence, too, like *Speak* by Laurie Halse Anderson, and *Crank* by Ellen Hopkins, and even *Scars*."

"That's true," Ms. Hirano says, nodding at Desi, "Although the majority of recent banned books are trans, queer, and Black, brown, and Indigenous. And while some book bans get attention, many books are just quietly removed from shelves, or outright not purchased because of book banning laws."

She looks around the room, recrossing her legs. "Do you think people should be able to tell you what you can't read? Do you think other students' parents, or even the government, should tell you that a book is off limits?"

"No way; it's fascist," Desi says.

"It's not fascist!" Gabby shouts. "It's protecting you from yourself. Protecting your innocence if you have any left."

"Oh, please—" Desi rolls their eyes.

"It is fascist, though," I say. "It's what they did in early Nazi Germany—ban and burn books, especially queer books." I have to stop for a breath.

"That's a lie!" Gabby yells. "You're just trying to make us look bad."

"You're doing that all by yourself," Desi mutters.

Zoey snorts.

Ms. Hirano holds up her hands, then points to me. "Were you finished?"

I shake my head. "Nazis burned the entire library at the Institute of Sexology which was researching and advocating for queer rights, as well as at least twenty thousand other books from around Germany. And they made laws against queer people, and stirred up hatred, which is happening now, too." The wheeze in my breath is loud.

I sit back, trying to breathe more lightly. I can't believe I said so much. It looks like the others can't, either. But one of the things I do when I'm in the hospital or sick at home is read. Reading has saved my sanity, kept me from drowning too deep in depression or anxiety about my health, even kept me from wallowing in self pity. Books have kept me company for as long as I can remember.

Jenna never got it—she thinks books are a chore—but I can tell Desi does. It makes me like them even more.

I wheeze again. I don't want to use my inhaler in front of the others, especially Desi, so I practice on breathing as quietly as I can without coughing, and don't speak for the rest of the period.

Desi catches up to me in the hall. "Hey," they say, nudging me. "Why'd you stop talking in class?"

I struggle to control my breathing. "Uh—I didn't want to get shouted down again."

Desi shakes their head. "You were awesome! You roasted Gabby with the truth." They clap my shoulder. "You gotta trust yourself more, you know? You knew way more than the others did." They grin at me, then walk off.

I wait until Desi's swallowed up by the crowd before I take a quick puff from my inhaler, my heart shuddering in my chest. Desi liked what I said! They even touched me. I imagine them leaning in closer, their brown eyes intent on mine. I wish I could believe they were interested in me, but Desi's so gorgeous in a loud, queer way, healthy and fit, and they're popular, unlike me.

I sigh, then cough. I've got to stop crushing on them; I just don't know how. I feel happier whenever I see them, and the world seems brighter, more full of possibilities. I just want to be around them. But lying to myself about how they might feel is only going to cause me heartache.

3

AFTER LUNCH I DUCK into a bathroom stall and use my inhaler again; my wheeze has become more audible and my lungs ache. But next period is gym; no way am I missing it when Desi's going to be there. I change fast and head out with the others.

"We're running track today, folks!" Mr. Taylor calls, his bright blue jacket, shirt, and shorts making his black skin gleam. "Let's go!"

Students around me cheer, but I cringe. Being outside in the pollen-laden air, especially on a humid day, is probably going to make my asthma worse. I trudge out with the others.

By the time I near the track, my chest hurts like my ribs are scraping my flesh with every breath, and the wheeze is loud. But I want to be able to do things like any other student. Especially because Desi's here.

I take another puff from my inhaler, then stuff it into my backpack and try to breathe slower as I walk toward the bleachers, hoping Mr. Taylor won't notice. I walk faster, shaking out my hands, the grass springy under my feet.

Out on the track a girl trips over her own feet and goes sprawling across the asphalt. Desi stops to help, the muscles in their arm flexing as they pull the girl up.

I can't stop watching them. They look so full of laughter and life, like they contain the sun inside their body and it shines out through the kindness in their eyes and smile, and their bronze skin. I'm drawn to their kindness and goodness, to the way they care about injustice, and the way they help others.

I dump my backpack onto the bleachers, run my fingers through my short brown hair, my fingertips skimming the shaved sides of my scalp, and start toward the track. Students are already running the circuit, doing laps, making it look easy and effortless. I long to be one of them—to be able to run without having to stop.

Mr. Taylor strides over. "You thinking of joining in today, Kate?"

I breathe in shallowly and smile. "Yeah, Mr. Taylor. I'm good."

He nods. Desi is coming around the track for another lap. I push forward and join them, matching my pace to theirs, the track firm beneath my feet. "Hey."

"Hey." Desi grins at me, sweat glistening on their skin. "I meant what I said earlier—you were awesome in English."

"You were, too," I say, trying not to gasp.

Desi grins at me wider.

I want to ask if they want to be friends, but faced with their confidence, the words stick in my throat.

"Isn't it great out here?" Desi asks.

"What?" I say, trying to keep my breathing easy. My chest tightens.

"You know—warm sun, bright blue sky, white clouds. Perfecto. Sure beats being stuck in a smelly gym."

For most people it does. But at least indoors I'm safe, as long as no one smokes, sprays aerosols, or uses heavy chemicals. It's hard for me to see the outdoors as beautiful when it so often messes with my breathing.

But they're right. "Yeah," I say. "It's nice."

"I wish we had class out here every day."

I can hear my wheeze again, louder than before. Desi must hear it, too. I think even the kid in front of us can; he turns to look. I try to suppress the sound, but that just makes me cough.

"Hey—you okay?" Desi asks, their forehead wrinkling as they

watch me.

It's getting harder to pull in air and my breath is coming in short gulps, now. "I'm fine," I say. I'm not, but if I stop now and get my inhaler, they'll just see me as the sick girl. But if I collapse on them that'll happen anyway.

If I don't stop the asthma attack from happening, visions will flood through me—horrific fractures of someone's life that'll come true if I can't make them believe me. Like Nevaeh. I knew she was going to die. But her breathing had gotten better and nobody listened. She had another attack that night—a fatal one. She was ten years old.

I can't get enough air. I slow down; I sound like a broken railway train.

I stop, hands on my knees, trying to breathe. My chest aches with the effort. *Stay calm. Breathe deeply and slowly*, I tell myself, desperately trying to suck in oxygen. But it's like I'm drowning. How could I have been so stupid, trying to run out here?

The world around me grows hazy, everything made up of tiny, moving dots of color that slowly reshape themselves. I fight it, dreading what I'll see, but the vision sharpens until I can't see anything else.

Jenna cowers against a wall, her shoulders hunched. "I'm sorry, Mason. Don't do this." Her voice breaks.

"You bitch. You're sorry?" Her husband slams his fist into her chest so hard she crumples against the wall, gasping.

My heart clenches. *Oh Jenna, why didn't you tell me?* I wheeze louder, my sight moving in and out, until I see both worlds at once. *Why does it have to be Jenna, when I've never been able to help anyone, not completely?*

"You've got asthma, right?" Desi says.

"Yes," I rasp through my wheezing.

"Where's your inhaler?" they ask.

I point to the bleachers. "Rainbow backpack." My lungs feel like they're filling up with phlegm. "Bleachers."

My vision grows hazy again.

Jenna struggles to stand. Mason punches her, knocking her to the floor like a ragdoll. He kicks her chest and stomach. Jenna curls up in a ball, trying to protect herself with her arms, but the blows keep coming.

Get up, Jenna; run away! But she won't. Despair tries to pull me under. I clench my fists, still wheezing. It doesn't matter if I've never been able to protect anyone else; I have to try. I can't let this happen to her. I've got to find a way to stop it.

Should I tell her I know, even if she doesn't believe how? Maybe this time will be different. Maybe she'll actually believe me. If he's hit her before, she has to know it's the truth. And maybe if she believes me it'll make a difference.

But what if my telling Jenna makes it worse? She's so private about Mason. I wheeze. But my not talking to her about it will for sure mean it'll happen the way I saw it. I have to tell her—even if she hates me for it. Better she hates me than gets so badly hurt.

I try to ground myself to get calm, noticing what I can hear (students running past, a few stopping to talk about me), what I can feel (hands on my soft cotton pants), what I can see (asphalt with painted lines beneath me, the hazy legs of the other students), what I can smell (cut grass, car exhaust). The attack's not bad yet, but that doesn't mean it won't get worse. I know how bad it can get—all those trips in an ambulance, the paramedics shouting, the ventilator breathing for me, my parents and Jenna crying....

Desi is running for my bag, calling for Mr. Taylor. Other kids stare as they run on the track, slowing when they get close to me the way cars do for an accident. More stop to watch me, my breath loud and raspy, my chest heaving. I wish they'd look somewhere else.

"Keep going round!" Mr. Taylor yells at them as he runs to me, his jacket flapping. "Breathe deeply, Kate," he says, lowering me to the ground. "Nice deep breaths."

"You think you can look at another man, you bitch!" Mason screams.

Jenna moans, clutching her stomach as she lies curled up on the floor, tears streaming down her cheeks. "I'm sorry! I have to talk to him; he's my boss."

Mason bends over and slaps her. "Don't lie to me!"

"I can fix it. I'll work less shifts."

"Fine," Mason says. "You know I never wanted you to work."

"But we need the money, baby."

"No we don't," Mason says, his face in hers.

I want to scream at Jenna to get away. I don't know if what I'm seeing is in the past or the future. But somehow I don't think it's happened yet.

Desi is back, my knapsack in their hands. "Where is it?" they say. "Where's your inhaler?"

I point to the front pocket, my breath rasping and whistling in my chest. Desi unzips the pocket, yanking out my inhaler. I shake it, then jam the mouthpiece into my mouth, press down, and breathe in. I hold my breath until I cough, and the wheezing starts again.

Mason hauls her up and slams her against the wall. "Why'd you take thirty dollars out of our account without asking me?"

Jenna shakes. "I'm sorry! They're having a baby shower at work for Shanice. I had to get her something."

"You swear it wasn't for your boss?"

"I swear."

Mason smashes his fist into a framed photo of our family: Jenna and me, stiff beside each other, Dad on Jenna's side and Mom on mine.

Glass shatters, raining down. Jenna cries out.
Mason grabs a shard of glass and presses it against Jenna's throat. A
bead of blood forms and trickles down her chest. "You can't keep doing
this to me, Jenna. I need you. You're the only one I've ever needed. You
can't look at other guys."
"I wasn't! I swear I wasn't."
Mason drops the glass. "Show me you love me."

She looked so vulnerable and terrified as she dragged her gaze up
to him. *Don't listen to him, Jenna! Don't trust him!*

My chest aches as I struggle to draw in air. I don't know how to
help Jenna. She acts like Mason is her knight in a shining pickup
truck. I've got to find a way to get through to her, stop letting her
pretend everything's okay and pushing me away.

I shiver. I've never had so many strong, clear vision fragments, one
after the other. But I've never had visions about Jenna, either.

Mr. Taylor rests his hand on my shoulder. "Nice, easy breaths," he
says. "You're okay, Kate. You'll be okay."

I'm still gasping and hacking like an old smoker, my chest heaving
in and out, my flesh tight against my ribs. Students slow down to
look every time they pass. Butterflies flutter above the flower beds,
floating gracefully on the air I struggle to inhale.

Desi hovers in front of me, their eyes wide, teeth biting their lower
lip. I don't want them seeing me like this, but I don't want them to
go, either.

I use the inhaler again. It's hard to wait between puffs when you
feel like you're suffocating.

My vision shifts, the world around me fading. Another scene
comes into focus.

A girl with bronze skin and brown eyes like Desi's sits hunched over
a desk in a bedroom, her dark hair limp and greasy, her black T-shirt
and sweatpants hanging off her. She stares at a tattered photo of a

*dark-haired woman smiling at a child—her—and a kid, a much
younger Desi, then crumples it up.*

*The girl lines up prescription bottles on her desk with shaking hands.
Then she picks up a glass of water, pours out a handful of pills, and
swallows. She takes another handful and swallows again, her throat
convulsing.*

I kneel there, horror making me cold. I've never seen a suicide
before—a suicide that hasn't happened yet. How can I stop this girl
from killing herself? I don't even know her. Yet her face is familiar.

The weight of two people's lives presses down on me as if their
bodies are piled on top of mine, making me so heavy I can barely
keep my head up. I cough. I have to do something.

I don't know the girl's name but I know she's connected to Desi
somehow. And I've seen her at school; she's a year or two ahead of
me. Normally I wouldn't have noticed her, but there was something
about her... I squint, trying to remember.

I see her face again—and then I know. A few months ago, someone
sent naked photos of her to all the students. She was bullied and
ostracized, straight girls treating her like she was toxic, and straight
boys leering at her, catcalling her, pressuring her to have sex with
them. I haven't seen her lately, but I didn't think anything about it;
it's a big school.

I wheeze once more, my neck tight. I can't let that girl die.

I've never seen visions about two different people at the same time.
I can't even protect one person. How am I going to protect two?

THE ATTACK IS EASING up now and my breath isn't so noisy and labored.

"Are you okay to get to the nurse's office with an escort?" Mr. Taylor asks. "Or do you need an ambulance?"

"I'm fine. It wasn't a really bad attack." But it wasn't mild, either. "I could stay out here with the class."

"No, you can't," Mr. Taylor says. "You know the protocol."

I sigh, the sound loud and whistling. I'm lucky the nurse, Mrs. Williams, is in today. Otherwise I'd have to go to the office and they'd phone Mom to pick me up—if they didn't call an ambulance first. "I can get to the nurse's." I stand, feeling shaky. Asthma attacks are exhausting. "Can Desi take me?" I say.

Mr. Taylor looks over at Desi, who nods. "Sure."

"Please—don't call my mom."

Mr. Taylor shakes his head. "I'm sorry, Kate; you know I have to. Parents have to be notified after every asthma attack."

Desi takes my arm and I let them, though I can walk just fine. We start off across the field toward the school. Its dark brick, small windows, and high wire fences remind me of a prison.

"You should've told me," Desi says, reproach in their voice.

"Told you—?" For a second I think they know what I've seen. I cough, the pain in my chest easing a bit more.

"That you weren't feeling well. I wouldn't have run so hard."

"I wanted to run with you."

Desi stops. "But that's not cool. I don't want to make you sick."

"You didn't. The weather can bring on an attack sometimes. Running, too. Lots of things can." My wheezing is getting lighter. Behind us, Mr. Taylor shouts at the students to run faster.

I glance at Desi out of the corner of my eye. We're far enough away from the others that no one can hear us. I have to say something. If I don't and the girl dies, I'll never forgive myself. But that doesn't make it any easier. The disbelief, the wondering about my sanity or my motives, the way people pull away from me, blame me—it all hurts. Desi might never talk to me again, might even look at me with hate in their eyes. But that girl—she must be important to Desi.

I take a shuddering breath and lick my dry lips. "Desi—do you have an older cousin who goes to our school? Or maybe a sister? Who might be...depressed?"

Desi stiffens beside me, their fingers clenching my arm. "A sister. Why?"

I briefly close my eyes. *I hate this part.* Desi will never see me the same way—if they ever come near me again. I've lost so many people this way. But I have to say something. "I think your sister is going to try to kill herself."

Desi jerks away from me, their mouth tight. "Why would you say that?" They jab their finger at me. "Why *the fuck* would you say that?"

I try to stand tall, taking another puff on my inhaler to make sure I don't have a relapse. "I'm sorry; I know it's a shock. But has she been depressed? Not sleeping, not showering or getting dressed?"

"Yes. But. How. Do. You. Know?" Their hands clench and unclench.

I swallow tightly. "I see things—visions—when I have an asthma attack. I know it sounds unbelievable, but I always have, and they always come true."

I wait for them to shove me, or turn away, or call Mr. Taylor. But they don't do any of those things. Instead their hands open, their shoulders loosen, and their mouth gets softer.

"You see things," they say without inflection.

"Yes." I cough, but it's reflexive. My breathing is almost normal again, although my chest aches. "I see the future, and sometimes the past. I wouldn't have said anything, but your sister—she was lining up pills on her desk."

"What pills?"

I can't believe they're still talking to me. This is where people usually freak out. I bite my lip. "Prescription bottles. A lot of them." I hesitate. "I think I recognized one—it was light purple, like Ambien. My dad takes it for insomnia."

"Ambien. Yeah. That's right," Desi says softly. They take my arm and we start walking across the field again. "Do you know when?"

I'm shocked they're asking that, and so casually, like they're taking me seriously. Like they actually believe me. Even my parents and sister don't do that.

I think back. I didn't see a computer screen showing a date. But her cell was face up on her desk. I concentrate hard, pulling the image back to me. "I think—it was the twenty-third of this month."

"Crap. That's Friday," Desi says. "I'll talk to her, get my nana to. We'll figure something out."

Chills run across my skin. They believe me! We might have a chance to save Inez. I shouldn't get my hopes up—but I have to try. "There's something else," I say. "She was staring at a torn photo of a woman. She crumpled it up before she took the pills."

"I'll bet it was our mamá," Desi says, running their fingers through their hair. "She left when we were little, around this time of year. Inez is older than me so she remembers her better. She's never gotten over it."

"I'm sorry," I say quietly.

We walk across the parking lot, past a group of students leaning against the fence smoking, their cigarette and weed smoke twisting and undulating above their heads like snakes. I try not to breathe until we pass them. Desi steers me toward the dull, scratched metal doors.

I walk slower. "Why do you believe me?"

Desi cocks one eyebrow. "Don't you want me to?"

"Of course! But people usually think I'm mentally ill when I tell them what I see. Or that I'm lying to get attention."

Desi looks at me, their eyes dark and serious. "People are too quick to dismiss what they don't understand, or what isn't their own experience."

I want to cry with relief. Desi has a more open mind than most people.

They smile crookedly. "My nana—she's a bit like you. She's got...a gift."

My heart skips in my chest, stealing my breath. I've never met anyone like me. "She's clairvoyant, too?"

"No, she's a médium psíquico. She talks to the dead."

"Oh." My shoulders slump. I should be glad; it's the first time I've heard of anyone even remotely like me. But she's not a seer. Just for a second, I'd thought I wasn't alone anymore.

Desi squeezes my arm. "I need to deal with this, make sure Inez is okay. But later, if you want, you can meet my nana. She'll talk to you."

"Thank you," I say, my eyes burning. I knew they were kind.

They pull open the heavy door and I stumble in, almost tripping over the concrete step. Desi catches my arm, the warm grip of their hand steadying me.

"Before we started track you were watching me," Desi says. "Was it because you saw my sister?"

My cheeks grow hot. "No. My asthma hadn't kicked in bad yet." I cringe inside, waiting for them to ask why I was watching them, but they don't. We walk down the empty hallway, passing classrooms full of students bent over their desks, their teachers droning on.

I glance at Desi to find them watching me, their eyes amused. "Well, this is it," they say, gesturing to the nurse's office.

My cell rings. I look at the screen, then roll my eyes. "My mom. Mr. Taylor must've called her already."

"You're lucky. I wish my mamá had cared so much."

"Let me know how your sister is, okay?"

"Sure. Give me your number and I'll text you mine."

I rattle it off, and they tap their cell. My phone pings.

"That's me," they say. "You see anything else, call. Okay?"

"Yeah."

They hand me my backpack, and turn to leave.

"Wait!" I say, slinging my backpack over my shoulder, my phone still ringing.

They turn back, eyebrows raised.

It's not fair to let them assume they can protect their sister just because I warned them. I swallow tightly. "I—I've never been able to protect anyone using my visions before."

Desi stiffens. "Never?"

I shake my head, then cough. "No one's ever believed me—except a kid no one listened to, and a suspicious cop who only got the girl back after she went through a lot of trauma."

Desi raises their chin, their brown eyes fierce. "Well, I believe you. My nana will believe you, and so will Inez. I'm gonna help her. I won't let her die."

I hope they're right. I pray they are.

"It's gonna be different this time," Desi says, shaking their head, their bangs falling into one eye. "You'll see."

"I hope so." For both Inez and Jenna.

Desi squints at me, pursing their mouth. "You don't believe me. Even more important, you don't believe in yourself."

My phone stops ringing. I bite my lip. "How can I when I've never been able to protect anyone?"

Desi frowns. "You're not given these visions for nothing. They're to help you make a difference," they say, throwing up their hands. "And you have me and my family who believe you now. Already that has changed things. Now you need to believe in you." They point at my chest. "You need to believe you can stop the bad things you see from happening." They step closer. "Do you believe?"

They are so close I can feel their warm breath on my cheek.

"I—I want to," I say.

Desi grabs both my hands. "You must," they say fiercely. "It gives your actions more power. Your visions, too."

I wonder how they can be so sure when they don't see visions themselves, and neither does their grandmother.

Desi's eyes darken. "My nana, she's helped many people because she believes in her ability, and what the dead tell her. To not believe is to turn your back on your gift." They let my hands go.

"I believe my visions," I say weakly.

They shake their head. "But you do not believe you can change them. You must believe you can. It'll help you actually do it. You must for Inez." They inhale deeply. "And already things are changing, yes? I believe your visions. My family will. And I believe in you."

They sound so fierce and sure of themself. I want to believe them. But how can I? Breath shudders in my lungs.

Desi takes a step back and thumps their chest. "I believe in me, too. And I am going to help Inez want to stay."

I hope they're right.

"You'll see," they say. "Even if you don't believe me now, you will. We'll save Inez, and that will change how you see your visions."

"Thank you," I whisper. My cell rings, and I jump.

Desi smiles crookedly. "It is I who should thank you."

My cell rings again, insistently. "I should answer that or she'll come tearing down here."

"Yeah, you should," Desi says, smiling sadly, then walks away.

I SIGH AND ANSWER the phone as I walk into the nurse's office, past all the familiar posters about the dangers of cigarette smoke, the importance of getting a flu shot, and how to prevent sun stroke. I'm here so often, I've memorized them all. "Hi Mom. I'm getting checked out by the nurse now."

"How bad was it?" Mom asks anxiously. "Did you use your inhaler?"

"I'm fine. It was just a mild attack." Well, it wasn't severe, anyway. "I took four puffs. It calmed down. I'm okay."

"I'll come pick you up."

"No! Let me stay the rest of the day; it's not that long. And I'll probably head over to Jenna's afterward. Besides, I thought you were showing a house."

Mrs. Williams, the school nurse, pokes her head out of her private office and waves at me, her long black hair in gorgeous locs, her rounded cheeks curving as she smiles. "Be right there," she mouths. She ducks back into her office, her keyboard clicking.

"You know I can reschedule," Mom says. "That's why I became a realtor—so I could be there when you need me."

"I'm okay, Mom, honest. Please let me stay. I've missed so much school already. It was just a little flare-up."

"You're sure?" Her voice wavers.

"Yes! I'm good now. And I haven't seen Jenna in weeks."

Mom sighs. "I want you home right afterward. And if you start wheezing again, call me immediately."

"Okay. I promise," I say, and disconnect. I sigh, a wheeze in my breath. I'm glad Mrs. Williams is the school nurse. She's always friendly and kind to me; I know her better than anyone else here. She never treats me like a burden or like she pities me, unlike some of the other teachers and students. And she walks like she feels good in her body and can take up space, even though our society is so racist and fat phobic. I wish I felt that comfortable with my own plumpness and queerness, and my psychic ability, too.

But I'm working on it. I touch my keychain—the plump flying pig with the delighted look on her face, doing the impossible...like me. Her plumpness looks beautiful and right, like she's just the way she's supposed to be. Maybe I'm the way I'm meant to be, too.

Mrs. Williams comes out of her office and looks at me sympathetically. "Another attack?"

"Yeah. But I'm all right now."

Mrs. Williams squints at me. "You're talking in full sentences and you don't have a loud wheeze. That's a good sign. But I can still hear it. I think you should stay here a while so I can keep an eye out for you."

She would. Mom is like the asthma liaison for the entire school, educating every teacher and staff member she can find to make sure they know how to help. She's so zealous that I think some of them are scared of her. Not Mrs. Williams, though. I sigh again, then cough. "Okay. But I need to call my sister."

Mrs. Williams wags her finger at me, but her brown eyes are smiling. "Go ahead. You're the only one here right now. But then I want you to rest. Come get me if it gets worse."

She retreats back into her office.

I walk into the tiny student room with its beige walls, industrial carpet, and fluorescent lighting, sit down on the padded bench, and speed dial Jenna.

"Jenna?" I don't know how to say this. I should probably wait until I'm with her in person. But I keep seeing Mason punch her, and her crumpling to the floor. "Are you all right?"

"Of course I am," Jenna says. "Why wouldn't I be?"

I grip my cell harder. "Well—are you and Mason all right? I mean, does he treat you okay?"

"Of course! Why would you ask that?" Jenna's voice is shrill and tight, but I can't stop.

"Has he ever hit you? Because if he has, you know you can come home any time. Mom and Dad would love to have you back."

"Where're you getting this from? Is this one of your hallucinations? I don't know what you think you saw, but we're good," Jenna says sharply.

My chest aches. Why won't she tell me the truth? And why won't she believe in my visions? I get her being defensive about Mason. But she's never believed me, even when she saw they turned out to be true. She just excuses it all as coincidence, or good instincts, or refuses to discuss it. And this time it's more important. This time it's about her.

My wheezing is getting louder again. I force myself to breathe slower. "I'm just worried about you." I cough.

"I'm fine," Jenna snaps. "Sounds like you should worry about yourself."

I wish I knew how to change the future. How hard I need to push. Unless Jenna *is* telling the truth and it's my visions that are lying. Mason has always seemed like a nice guy, doting on Jenna, giving her gifts, always wanting to know about her day. Maybe my visions aren't always right; maybe they're just one likely outcome, an outcome I can try to change. Maybe it hasn't happened yet.

My wheezing gets raspier. "Could I come over after school?"

"Why?" Jenna asks.

"I had another asthma attack. You know how Mom gets. She'll be hovering all over me like a fly on dog poop."

Jenna snorts.

"If I breathe wrong she'll shove my puffer in my mouth." I gasp for breath. "And I haven't seen you in weeks."

"How bad was it? Do I need to get your nebulizer out?"

"No, it wasn't that bad. You know the school has to call her every time it happens. So can I come?"

"Sure—as long as you stop bad-mouthing Mason."

"Okay," I say. But I know I can't leave it like that. I have to find out the truth. Because if Mason really is beating Jenna, I have to help her.

I hang up and stare at my cell, my breath rasping louder. Somehow, I have to help Jenna escape abuse, and stop Inez from killing herself.

I laugh-cry, my shoulders shaking. I've never been able to protect anyone, and now I have to save my own sister and Desi's, too.

I cough hard.

I can't fail this time.

6

JENNA YANKS OPEN HER apartment door after my first knock, like she's been waiting for me. "Are you ever going to wear regular glasses? Those rainbow ones are so loud."

"Nope. That's kinda the point." I hug her. She hesitates, then hugs me back. It hasn't even been a year since she eloped, but it feels a lot longer. Every time I see her, she seems farther away.

I step back and study her face. Shadows under her eyes show faintly beneath her careful makeup, and her mouth has that tight look she gets when she's trying to hold in emotion. And there's a faint red spot on her neck. She holds her body stiffly like it's hurting her, but when she sees me looking, she straightens up and smiles.

I touch her neck. "What's this?"

"Just a mosquito bite. You know how they love me."

I squint. It could be. But I don't think it is. "Jen—you okay?" I ask.

"Of course. How are *you*? You're the one who had the asthma attack."

I hope she's telling the truth. But that's not what my gut is telling me.

She turns and walks off toward the kitchen and I follow. "You want something to drink?" she asks with her back to me.

"Just water."

She gets a glass out of the cupboard.

"How's your stomach?" I ask. "You feeling any better?"

"It was nothing," Jenna says quickly. She turns on the tap, fills the glass, and hands it to me. "You sound better. You're not wheezing anymore."

I take a sip of water. "I told you I was fine."

Jenna nods. "Yeah, like that time you kept telling the babysitter not to call Mom—and then we had to rush you to the hospital? Or when you tried to muffle your coughing by putting a towel under the door? And you wonder why Mom and I double check."

I slam my glass down on the scuffed counter. "I hate going to the hospital! It hurts when they put the breathing tube in."

"I know," Jenna says, her eyes going soft. "I'm sorry." She sets her own water glass down on the counter next to the nebulizer she keeps for me.

"I told you I didn't need that!" I say.

"We just *had* this conversation." Jenna studies me. "But yeah, you seem okay."

I roll my eyes. "Thanks, Mom." But deep down I'm glad she had it ready, just in case.

Jenna checks her watch.

"You have somewhere you need to be?" I ask.

"No; I just like to have things ready for Mason when he comes home. But I have a few hours yet."

I don't understand her catering to Mason like she doesn't have a life of her own. It's not something Mom ever did with Dad, at least not to this extent. "Can't he make his own dinner for once?"

Jenna presses her lips tightly together. "He works hard all day."

"So do you."

"My job's only part-time." Jenna waves her hand. "It's nothing. So why are you *really* here?"

With the way she reacted before when I asked her about Mason, I need to tread carefully. "I need to hide from Mom before she smothers me."

"Yeah, that must be *so* hard," Jenna says, a bite in her voice like chili pepper inside sugar.

I cross my arms over my chest. "You try being under a microscope twenty-four hours a day, having her watch your breathing, your color, and monitoring everything you do. I can't even cough without her running for my inhaler or my air-flow meter."

"She loves you," Jenna says, but it sounds like she means the opposite.

"She loves you, too," I say. "She cried for weeks after you left. She misses you; she says she never sees you any more, not without Mason."

Jenna holds up her hand like a traffic cop. "She had plenty of time to see me when I lived at home, but she was always too busy taking care of you. Besides, Mason and I are married now. That's what couples do—spend time together."

"You can do things on your own, too. You can spend time with your family."

"Mason *is* my family."

My stomach tightens. "So are we. We'll always love you, no matter what."

"Sure."

I bite my lip. "Are you sure things are okay with you and Mason?"

"Yes!" Jenna leans her hands behind her on the counter, her shoulders hitching up. "I'm a lot happier than I was at home. Mason pays attention to me. He really loves me."

"Mom and Dad paid attention to you," I say, frowning.

Jenna laughs—a short, hard bark. "No. They gave *you* all the attention. You were the one who always needed it, not me. I was healthy, so I didn't matter."

"Of course you mattered!"

"No." Jenna pushes away from the counter. "Not the way you did. You could've died if they didn't monitor you right. Mom worried about you every minute of every day. Even when she talked to me, she was distracted."

"That's not true," I whisper. But her words hit me like a brick to my gut. No wonder Jenna hates me sometimes. "I'm sorry. She *is* obsessed with my health. But at least you always had Dad. The two of you did everything together. I hated getting left out of everything because I was sick."

"I know," Jenna says. "But you being sick affected us all. I didn't get to be a normal teen, either. I couldn't have hair spray, or perfume, or even nail polish, for God's sake! And I couldn't smoke, not even weed! Mom was always too hyper alert. I couldn't do anything that would set off your asthma. It was like living in jail."

I hug my stomach. "It wasn't fun for me, either. And it's not like I could stop it. Do you think I chose to be sick? It's awful."

"Yeah, well, at least you got Mom's attention."

And she got Dad's. I stare at the tile floor. I don't want to get into this with Jenna. It's how all our conversations end up now—talking about how my asthma affected her. The guilt feels like parasites eating away at me.

I shake myself. This isn't why I came. I need to find out what's really going on with Jenna, and not let her divert me the way she usually does. I look up.

Silent tears are rolling down Jenna's cheeks. She looks so much younger when she cries. More vulnerable. Approachable.

I rush over and hug her. "I'm sorry. I love you."

Jenna wraps her arms around me. "I'm sorry, too." She rests her cheek on top of my head. "I know it's hard to always be sick. I used to see you watching me when I was out playing. You looked so sad and alone."

I lean back to look at her. Her mouth is as soft as her eyes. If I'm going to get the truth from her, it's probably now. "I know you don't believe my visions. But I 'saw' Mason punch and kick you. If he's ever—"

Jenna pulls away. "He hasn't." She straightens up, her mouth tight again, and presses a hand to her throat. "Why would you even say that?"

"But if he ever does, you know you can come home any time you need to. We all miss you. And we want you to be safe—"

"I *am* safe. And happy," Jenna says, holding her head high, looking down her nose at me. "I think you're just jealous someone loves me so much."

Jealous? I stare at her, opening then shutting my mouth. I don't know how to get through to her.

The apartment door slams. "Hey, babe!" Mason calls. "Where are you?"

"In the kitchen with Kate," Jenna calls. "You're home early!"

Mason strides in smelling like cigarettes, a bouquet of flowers in his huge, grimy hand. I breathe shallowly; I don't want to have another attack.

"I got a buddy to cover me. I couldn't stop thinking of you, sweet thing." He grabs Jenna, lifting her off the ground as she squeals, and kisses her—long and deep.

I look away.

Jenna giggles and swats his arm. "Be good. My sister's here."

"I'm always good," Mason says. He sets her down and hands her the flowers, the cellophane crinkling. "And I got you your fave chocolate," he says, pulling out a candy bar from his pocket, and handing it to her. He leans in close. "I love you, babe. Whatever you want to do tonight, we will." He turns to me. "Hey, Kate. You have another attack?"

"Uh—yeah." How did he know that?

Mason takes off his stained baseball cap—part of his uniform at the gas station—and tosses it onto the counter. "Don't worry about it. You'll grow out of it."

Right. Because he knows so much more than all the specialists I've seen, the long parade of doctors. The thousands of hours of research my mom has done. I grit my teeth.

Jenna's arranging the flowers in a vase. "They're beautiful, honey," she says and looks triumphantly at me.

"Just like you, babe." He puts a finger under her chin, lifting her face up. "Have you been crying?"

"No, it's nothing," Jenna says quickly.

Mason narrows his eyes and turns to me. "I think it's time you went home, Kate."

I glance at Jenna, but she just looks away. "Okay," I say quickly. "I'll show myself out."

Mason's been super protective of Jenna ever since they started dating. It's hard to believe he could do what I saw.

But I know one way to be sure. I cut through the living room and walk over to the side table with the photo of Jenna, Mom, Dad, and me, all crowded together on the porch swing, laughing in the evening light. It looks perfect.

I take a step closer.

The glass is gone. It's just a bare photo stuck in the frame.

I look down. Fragments of glass are lodged in the crack between the molding and the wall.

Goosebumps rise on my skin. What I saw was real.

I WALK HOME SLOWLY, pacing myself, not wanting my asthma to flare up again. Desi's right; there's got to be a way I can help. Otherwise why would I get these visions?

So if Jenna won't tell me the truth about Mason, how do I help her get safe? Could I convince her to come for a visit? Will she listen to our parents, to Dad, if she won't listen to me? Or does she not want to admit the abuse to them, either?

I yank out my cell phone, search partner abuse, tap open an article, and scan it quickly. The way Mason came home with flowers and chocolate, all charm and affection, acting like everything is okay—that's part of the cycle of abuse and forgiveness. And Jenna going along with it can be her wanting to believe that Mason will never be violent or abusive again. That she made the right decision to be with him, especially with all the harsh criticism she got from teachers, friends, and neighbors after she eloped. And maybe there's fear mixed in there, too.

I read about how to help victims. Listen and believe them—but she won't talk to me. Encourage them to think about safety and build a safety plan. Help them find domestic violence support services.

I search for domestic violence shelters. There's a few in our area. I take screenshots in case Jenna ever admits what's happening. At least

Mason wouldn't be able to find her there. Or maybe she could just talk to one of the counsellors, see that it's not her fault and she's not the only one this has happened to. But I know that I can't offer her that yet; it'd push her away.

I rub my face. This may be a lot harder than I thought and take longer than I want it to. Jenna's not even opening up to me. But if Mason keeps escalating, do we have time for a slow approach?

I shiver. I'll just have to keep working on her trusting me.

Then there's Inez.

Tiny drops of rain gently fall around me; it's almost like walking through a cleansing mist. I lift my face to the sky, looking past the houses, revelling in the soft caress of rain. It's a soothing, welcome distraction. I hope it'll wash away the pollen from the air—unlike a thunderstorm that can break up pollen and make it harder to breathe.

I don't know if I did enough for Inez, just warning Desi. I know they'll take it seriously, and talk to Inez. But will that be enough? When someone's struggling that hard, when they feel that hopeless, they usually need a lot of support—often more than just their family.

Should I say that? But I don't know Inez, not personally, and I barely know Desi. What if it pushes them away? Rain slides down my face like tears.

The few times I was so sick and miserable that I didn't want to be here, I needed hope that things would get better. And someone to listen to me with love and compassion. And escape, too, into my favorite books.

I scroll down to Desi's number, then text: **Inez may need to know that things can get better. And she may need someone else to talk to, besides you and your nana.**

I wait, holding my breath, then have to cough for air. I tap out another message: **Maybe a helpline? Or a therapist?**

Maybe, Desi texts back. **With her now.**

My body lightens. They wrote me back—and they're taking it

seriously. Maybe it'll be different this time. But I'm so afraid to hope.

The sidewalk glistens with rain, cars rushing by in the road, making a shushing noise on the wet asphalt. The rain is falling harder now, making little puddles on the sidewalk, rain drops falling in expanding circles, flattening my hair to my scalp.

I shiver as the rain soaks my clothes. Mom won't be happy. I keep walking, my jeans heavy and wet like the worry weighing me down. I couldn't get through to Jenna. Why do I think Desi will be able to get through to Inez? I'm stuck on how to help them both. I scurry up the walkway to our house.

My phone pings.

Don't give up, Desi texts. **I'm not.**

I shiver harder. It's like they read my mind.

I open the front door and try to sneak in, but Mom rushes over like she's been waiting for me.

"Any more trouble breathing?" Mom studies my face intently.

"No, I'm fine," I say.

She touches my hair. "You're soaked. Get upstairs and into dry clothes this instant. And keep your inhaler with you."

I try not to roll my eyes. Sudden weather changes can trigger an asthma attack, but this wasn't a thunderstorm. "It was just a little rain. I walked home slowly, I didn't exert myself—" except in gym— "And I had my cell out in case I needed to call you."

I must've laid it on too thick because Mom's forehead wrinkles and she moves closer, leaning in like she's listening to me breathe.

I try to breathe slow and steady, no wheeze.

"Did something happen?" Mom asks. "Something to upset you?"

Right, because that can be a trigger, too. Sometimes it feels like my whole life is about avoiding anything that could set off my asthma. Or omitting details about it to Mom. "I'm fine. But I want to talk to you both at dinner." Because Jeanna is not fine.

8

"I'm telling the truth!" I say, pushing my half-full plate of spaghetti away. It's as yummy as always, garlicky and packed with spinach, onions, and chickpeas in the tomato sauce, cheese grated on top, but my stomach feels too hard and tight, and I'm starting to wheeze.

"Did you *see* it happen?" Dad asks around his mouthful of pasta. "Did you actually see Mason hit her? Other than in your imagination?"

I knew they wouldn't believe me. "I didn't imagine it!" I say. "I told you, I saw it...in a vision."

"Not the visions again," Mom says, setting her fork down. "I understood it when you were little; you needed a distraction from being sick. But you're sixteen, now, Kate. You need to be more responsible and mature."

"I'm not making it up!" I say, wheezing harder. I need more details, something that will make them believe me. If Jenna won't talk to me, how can I convince them unless I have another vision?

"Take a breath," Mom says, pulling her chair closer to mine. "Breathe in slowly."

"Elizabeth, give her some space." Dad says, tearing off a hunk of garlic bread. "Let her deal with it on her own. Babying her isn't going to help her grow out of it."

"You've heard the doctors; people don't just grow out of asthma," Mom snaps. "They might stop showing symptoms for a while, but they'll always be asthmatic. And you know how bad it can get if we don't intervene. Have you forgotten all those trips to the hospital?"

"I'm fine," I say loudly, trying not to wheeze. "But Jenna isn't."

"What do you mean?" Mom asks.

"I told you. Mason's beating her."

"Breathe slowly, honey. We're trying to understand."

I'm wheezing louder, my chest tight and heavy. Why don't they ever believe me? "It's not hard to understand! He's abusing her."

"Did Jenna tell you that?" Dad asks.

"No. But victims often hide it!"

"Honey, calm down," Dad says. "You know Mason is not my favorite person, but if something like this were happening, Jenna would tell me."

"Right, because she *used* to tell you everything," I say. "But that was before Mason! You've seen how he's always with her whenever she visits. Do you even get time alone with her anymore?"

Dad sits back. "She has her own family now."

Mom plays with her watch, unbuckling it and then buckling it back up again. She knows I'm right—Jenna has grown more and more distant since she and Mason got together.

"She's still family," I say. "And she needs us."

"Jenna and I talk every week," Dad says, winding more pasta around his fork. "She knows I'll be there if she needs me. You can't let yourself get worked up like this; you know it just makes your asthma worse."

Maybe that's not such a bad thing if it helps me prove Jenna's in danger. But I hate struggling for air, feeling like I might die. Knowing I can.

"I'm telling you the truth." I scrape back my chair and stand, wheezing. "When are you going to start believing me?" I wheeze louder, my airways squeezing tight, and then I'm gasping.

Mom already has my spare inhaler out and primed. She pushes it into my hand and I squeeze down, inhaling as deep as I can before I wheeze again.

The living room grows fuzzy, Mom and Dad becoming hazy spots of color and light. I fight it but I'm still pulled deeper, my pulse hammering in my neck, the room blurring in front of me, the vision sharpening.

Mason walks down a long beige hall with a man in a white lab coat. "I'm really worried about my wife's sister, Kate," Mason says, holding his baseball cap in his hand. "She thinks she sees the future every time she has an asthma attack. I don't know if she's hallucinating, or psychotic, or what. Do you have any idea what could make her think that's happening?"

The doctor rubs his chin. "Well, it could be something as simple as hypoxia, a lack of oxygen to the brain during her attacks. Or it could be any number of mental health conditions triggered by the stress she experiences during her attacks. But I'd have to examine her to be sure."

Hypoxia? A lack of oxygen? Mental health issues? Is this my brain's way of telling me that my visions really are hallucinations? Or am I seeing Mason's actual conversation with a doctor about me?

Mom's rubbing my back, talking to me in that calm voice she uses when I have my attacks. It always makes me feel like I can breathe easier before I actually can. Dad's sitting there stiffly, watching us, clenching his fork. I take another puff from my inhaler.

"My wife's so worried about her sister that she's not sleeping," Mason says, turning his baseball cap around in his hands. "So if I bring Kate in, you'll see her?"

"If you can manage to bring her in, I'll fit her into my schedule," the doctor says. "But from what you've said, it doesn't sound like she'll want to come voluntarily."

"I'll find a way to get her here," Mason tells him.
"Then I'll see her."
Mason clasps the doctor's hand. "Thank you, doctor! You don't know how much I appreciate this."

It's hard to believe Mason would do that; he's never been anything but nice to me. But he *is* overprotective of Jenna. And there's a tiny part of me that's never felt quite sure about him—but maybe that's because he took Jenna away from me. When I do see her he never wants me to stay long, and always finds a way to get me to leave. Or maybe he's right and I am hallucinating.

But the glass in the frame was smashed. Doesn't that prove my visions are real? Unless I'd subconsciously noticed it on my last visit and the vision was my mind's way of trying to make sense of it. But Desi believes my visions.

Air starts to come easier now. I gasp it in.

"Getting better?" Mom asks, rubbing my back.

I nod and sink back onto my seat, my legs rubbery and weak like they get sometimes after an attack. Two attacks in one day are a lot. Mom hovers over me for a moment, then sits, too.

Dad leans forward. "You okay now, Kate-girl?"

I nod.

"Good. That's good." Dad leans back and straightens his tie. "Listen, you've got to learn to control your asthma, even when something upsets you. Because there's always going to be things that upset you in life."

I'd like him have to struggle to breathe and see how he copes. I stab at my spaghetti with my fork. "I haven't had an attack for a while until today." Yeah, like maybe a whole week.

"Your mom and I are on your side," Dad says, patting his mouth with a napkin. "No matter what you do, we love you. But it's Jenna's word against yours on this. And if your imagination has gotten the better of you, or you've somehow misunderstood, it's better to let us know now, before things go too far."

I clench my fist. What's too far? Jenna ending up in the hospital, or worse?

"I'm telling the truth." I stand. "I'm going to lie down. I'm tired."

"Kate—" Mom starts to get up.

"Let her go," Dad says, waving his hand.

I climb the stairs to my room and slam my door closed.

"Leave it open!" Mom calls. "I want to know if you need me in the middle of the night. And don't forget your last dose of medicine!"

I open my door a crack, then flop down onto my bed. My "Keep Calm and Breathe Deeply" poster that Dad bought stares mockingly at me. I pull out my cell and text Desi. **My parents don't believe my visions. It makes me doubt them.**

My phone vibrates almost immediately. **Don't doubt! You were right about Inez. She's thinking of suicide.**

God. I'm sorry.

No, it's good; at least she's talking to us. I hope it's enough. Hope we caught it in time.

I hope so too. But keep a watch on her. Keep reminding her of reasons to live.

We will; believe me. What visions don't your parents believe?

I frown, biting my lip. It's a big thing to tell someone. But I told them about Inez; they might as well know about Jenna. **That my sister's husband beats her.**

That's serious. You've got to do something.

My parents don't believe it. Jenna denies it. What else can I do?

Call the cops.

I go cold. I can't go through that again. My parents can't, either. I see the flashing lights, the officers' suspicious looks, hear the radios squawking. **I can't.**

Why not? You're white—they'll treat you better. And if it

could save Jenna...

I swallow tightly. There's one detective I could maybe trust. But I see my father's grim face, his haunted eyes. I can't risk it, not again. **It's just not an option.**

Okay. We'll brainstorm tomorrow.

Thanks. Night, I text.

Night.

I feel calmer knowing Desi believes me, knowing we'll figure this out together. At least I've got one person on my side, one person who knows I'm not trying to manipulate anyone or make things up.

I smile up at my ceiling. Desi is so cute. I wonder if they'd ever be willing to go out with someone like me. Someone who'd have to cancel plans last minute, who'd make them worry.

I flash back to a few years ago, when I'd crept out to the landing, peering down through the banister to listen to Jenna shout.

Jenna's face is red, her hands clenching and unclenching. "I don't care if she had another attack!" *she screams.* "This was my try out. It was important to me! And you were both supposed to be there for once!"

"Your dad was there," *Mom says.* "What did you want me to do, let her die?"

"Yes!" *Jenna screams.* "At least we could have a normal life again, without the two of you always scared and distracted."

"You don't mean that," *Dad says.*

"Yes, I do," *Jenna says, tears streaming down her cheeks.* "It's not like she has any kind of life anyway."

A whimper escapes my throat.

Jenna looks up to see me at the top of the stairs, her eyes widening.

Mom looks up, too. "Honey," *she says, starting towards me.*

Jenna slams out the front door, Dad chasing after her.

I shake my head to clear it from the memory. Jenna's right; Mom was never there for her. But Dad was. I always envied their closeness, the way they had things to do and talk about that weren't about being sick. Little jokes and code phrases between them that I was excluded from. I may have had most of Mom's attention, but it was all about my asthma, not me. Not what I care about or who I am or who I hope to be.

I sigh and push out my breath, wheezing slightly. I think Jenna had the better deal. If I could trade places with her and be healthy and strong I would; I don't think she'd ever choose to trade places with me. Most people who have their health seem to take it for granted. But Jenna's seen how hard it is.

There's a knock on my door. Mom pokes her head in. "How's your breathing?"

"Fine. The inhaler worked." I smooth out my bedspread. "I'm sorry."

Mom walks in and sits down beside me on my bed. "What're you sorry for? It's not your fault you have asthma."

"I don't like it when you and Dad fight."

Mom squeezes my leg. "We just have different beliefs about how to help you. But we both love you. You know that, don't you?"

"Yeah, I know."

"Okay, then." Mom pats my leg and stands. "Don't forget to take your meds before bed."

"Yeah, yeah," I say.

Mom closes my door part way.

I pick up my cell again, staring at the texts. Desi wants to help me figure this out. I hope they'll still want to spend time with me after the crisis with Inez is over. Hope I'm not just a curiosity to them. But they don't seem like that. There's a kindness to them, a deep compassion, that I don't sense in most other people. A sensitivity that I'm drawn to. I wonder if they've had a hard life, too, or if they're just naturally kinder.

Even when they're correcting people on their pronouns for what must be the thousandth time they're patient—except when they're dealing with transphobes and homophobes. My first day back at school after months of being homeschooled last year, they were the only one who welcomed me, who even talked to me. Not that they likely remember. But even then, their warm brown eyes, wide smile, and kind voice made me want to be near them.

The rumble of my parents' voices downstairs is comforting. I take off my glasses, lean my head back against my pillow and close my eyes.

I wake up in the middle of an asthma attack, my lungs straining for air.

9

I SIT UP GASPING, trying to breathe. It feels like somebody's stitched my throat shut.

I kick off my blanket, fumble for my inhaler and suck in hard, trying to keep my hands from trembling. Panic only makes it worse, but it's hard to stay calm when I can't breathe. I know I could die. I cough harder.

My room grows fuzzy, colors and shapes rearranging themselves to show me a different scene.

Mason presses Jenna up against the wall, his arm rammed against her throat, cutting off her air. "Your sister is ruining everything. You've got to stop her—or I will."

Jenna shakes her head, gagging, clawing at his arm.

Mason loosens his grip. "Well?"

"Mason, you're scaring me," Jenna says, her voice a rasp. She massages her neck.

I cough. I don't like where this is going.

Mom comes running in, her nightgown rustling. She flicks on the light and sits on my bed, rubbing my back. "You've taken a puff?"

I nod, coughing harder. I don't have enough air to talk.

"It's not helping enough, is it?" Mom grabs my nebulizer from the side of the bed, snaps open a vial of medication and dumps it in the cup, hooking it up to the hose. I cough and cough, praying for air. Mom turns on the nebulizer. I can hear the hum over my wheezing. When I see the misty spray of the medication escaping, I grab the mask and slap it onto my face, trying to breathe through the coughing.

"Okay. You're okay. Just breathe deeply," Mom says.

Dad comes to stand in the doorway wearing just his pajama bottoms. He rubs his face, his hair sticking up, his other hand tight against the doorframe.

Dad blurs even more in front of me.

"I'm scaring you?" Mason steps back, fists clenched. "You should be scared of your freak of a sister. She's trying to break us up."

"Just leave her alone, Mason."

"I'm your husband!" Mason roars. He slaps her so hard, her head snaps back. She opens her mouth, but no sound comes out.

Mason slaps her again, his smartwatch flashing, reflecting the light. "You put your sister over me?" He grabs her head and smashes it against the wall again and again. When he stops, Jenna slides limply to the floor, her eyes wide and staring, her face still.

"Jenna! No! Speak to me, Jenna!"

Mason cradles her head and rocks her, sobbing, but she doesn't move.

Oh my god. He *killed* her!

My lungs ache like they've been turned inside out. I cough, trying to breathe. I can't let him kill her—unless he already did. I've got to find out when this vision happens. But how?

My thoughts race. His smartwatch! I've got to see it. Got to get back into that vision!

I've never done that before, intentionally gone back into a vision. I don't even know if forcing it will work, but I've got to try.

I force a cough, then another, pushing the medication out of my lungs, focusing on Mason slapping Jenna's face.

Nothing. The attack's easing off. I cough harder, trying to see Mason snapping Jenna's head back.

"Breathe," Mom says anxiously.

Guilt floods me. And then I'm back in Jenna's apartment.

Mason slaps her face again, his smartwatch flashing in the light.

I focus on the vision so hard it blurs. *"Slow down!"* I scream at it—and it does, Mason's arm inching forward, his smartwatch visible, but not the full face. *"Pause! Stop!"* I scream, my chest heaving, pain searing through my brain, and the vision halts, hovering in front of me like a 3D photo. I stare at the image, willing it to turn until I can read the watch face, and it does. *Two forty-five p.m. Friday.* I did it! But shit—which Friday? This Friday? It's Tuesday already! That's Jenna and Inez both dying on the same day. Maybe that's the reason I saw them both?

"Kate!" Mom cries. "Breathe!"

I gulp air, pain stabbing my lungs like broken glass. The mist fills my mouth and nose. Mom rubs my back. Even though I usually want her to stop hovering, right now I'm glad she's here.

I can feel the medication working. My lungs ease a little, clench less—but every breath hurts. I suck in as much medication and air as I can.

I didn't know I could do that—relive a vision, slow it down, even turn it to see another angle. It's amazing. But it's made such a deep pain in my chest, I almost don't want to breathe. I *had* to worsen my attack to save Jenna. But I never want to do that again.

The medication sputters out and I take off the mask. I breathe in tentatively and only cough a little. I slip my glasses on, and rub my aching chest.

"You had me worried for a while there," Mom says.

"I'll go make you some hot water with lemon and honey," Dad

says, smacking my door frame. "That always helps your throat."

"Thanks," I croak as he leaves. I turn to Mom. "I forgot to take—" I inhale raspily, "—my night meds." My voice is hoarse and throaty from all that coughing.

"That's not like you," Mom says, her eyebrows furrowing.

"I was so tired—" I take a raspy breath, "after the other attack," I breathe in, "I just fell asleep." I cough, then rub my chest. "And...I was worried." With good reason!

"About Jenna?"

"Yes."

Mom sighs and clasps my hand in hers. "You really believe Mason is hurting her?"

"I know he is!" I cough again.

"Deep breaths," she tells me. "Don't go getting yourself all upset again." Mom squeezes my hand. "Okay. I'll invite Jenna and Mason over for Friday night. Your dad can get Jenna on her own and talk to her."

Friday dinner will be too late. "Thank you," I whisper. "But could we do sooner?"

Mom shakes her head. "You know Jenna tells your dad more—and he's on a tight work deadline. Friday is only a few days away."

I know she doesn't really believe me, but at least she's trying. But it's not enough. I need to talk to Jenna again. "Yeah."

Mom squeezes my shoulder. "So you'll stop worrying, now?"

I shake my head. "I can't, Mom. I know you don't believe my visions—but I do." At least I do right now. And Desi does. Desi. We've got to figure out how to help Inez, too.

"I know you do." Mom kisses my forehead. "And if something is really happening, Jenna will tell us. Now get some sleep. We can talk about this more tomorrow." She turns off my nebulizer and stands. She's got that army-sergeant look about her, now: firm, rigid, and controlled.

"Talk after school?"

"You're not going to school, missy," Mom says, wagging her finger at me. "Not after three attacks in one day!"

"I have to! Please? I have my inhaler," I gasp-cough. "I promise I'll remember all my medication—"

"Why do you *have* to?" She sits back down.

I need to see Desi. Need to plan out how to help Inez and Jenna. If I stay home, Mom will be in and out all day. She'll overhear what we say, and she'll worry, maybe even try to stop us. And we only have until Friday to figure this out.

I go for the truths I don't normally tell her. "I'm out so much, it's like I don't belong there." I cough. "And there's someone I like..."

"Ah," Mom says, smiling. "Who's the girl?"

At least she accepts that I'm queer. Dad still tries to pretend I never came out to them, though when I force the issue he acknowledges my queerness. "They're a nonbinary lesbian. And they're so kind, Mom."

"And cute, I'll bet," Mom says.

My cheeks burn. "Yeah," I mumble.

"So—nonbinary means...they're not a girl or a boy?" Mom asks, scrunching up her forehead. I can tell she's read up on it, or heard about it, at least.

"Yeah, some people see it that way," I say, coughing again. "They don't fit into the Western idea that there are only two genders, woman or man." I suck in a wheezing breath. "They might feel like they're another gender, a blend of girl and boy or other genders," I cough, "Or they might not feel like they have any gender." I've been reading up on it, too.

"I think I get it," Mom says. She smooths back my hair. "Well, they'll still be there when you get back on Wednesday."

I bunch up my bed sheet. "But it's so much harder every time I'm out. No one talks to me. I'm the sick girl who misses school all the time, and wheezes when she's there. I hate it."

"I know you do," Mom says, her eyes tearing up.

"And I never get to have any kind of a normal life. But Desi said they wanted to see me tomorrow. Not a date, just...to talk." I cough. "So please let me go to school. I'll be careful. If I have an attack, I'll call you and you can take me home."

"Desi, huh?" Mom pats my leg. "We'll see. I'll check your peak air flow in the morning. If it's in the yellow or red zones, you're staying home. If it's green, you can go."

"But it's yellow so often! You know I can still be okay."

"We'll see," Mom says. She kisses my forehead. "Rest now."

I nod.

"And call me if you need me," she says.

"Thanks, Mom," I say, reaching for her hand. I don't think I tell her that enough. Her hovering gets on my nerves—but I wouldn't be alive if she hadn't driven me to the hospital many times, or pumped me full of medication when I couldn't do it myself.

Mom looks down at our clasped hands, her eyebrows raised. "You want me to stay? You not feeling good?"

I shake my head. "I'm okay." I suck in air. "Just—I appreciate everything you do for me. Everything you've done. I know I wouldn't be here without you. And I know I take up a lot of your time and energy." Deep wheezing breath. "Probably too much."

Mom's eyes fill with tears. "Oh honey, don't say that."

"But it's true."

Mom takes a shaky breath and squeezes my hand before letting go. "I've never regretted anything I've done for you," she says fiercely. "And I never will. You're my child. I love you. I want you to live. To be healthy and happy and well."

I nod, my eyes watering, too. "But you missed out—" wheezy inhale, "On things with Jenna. She resents me for it."

"Oh honey, she understands. We all had to make sacrifices. And you've suffered most of all."

She doesn't see it—how angry Jenna is. How she left to get away from this, to get away from me. The words clog my throat, and I cough again.

Mom smooths my forehead with her cool hand. "Jenna loves you," she says. "We all do. Don't ever forget that. Now let your worries go."

Like it's that easy.

She waits, arching one eyebrow.

I nod.

"Good," she says. "Now go back to sleep." She leaves, keeping my door open.

I'm too jumpy to rest or even to read. I pull out my cell phone, tap open my current favorite word game Letter Quest and start finding words to defeat the monsters. I'm grateful Nurse Sato got me into word games to calm me down after a really bad attack. I focus on finding one word, then the next, before my character loses. I hope between Desi and I we can figure out how to save Jenna and Inez before their time runs out.

10

Mom watches me closely as I rush through breakfast and my asthma meds. I know she's itching to tell me to stay home. I take a deep breath, put my peak flow meter between my teeth, my lips closing around it, and blow as hard and as fast as I can. I do this twice more, then hold out my peak flow meter to Mom. "See? Pretty good! It's closer to green than to red."

"Uh huh," Mom says, pursing her lips.

"And I already took my meds. I'll be fine. I promise." I clasp my hands together like I'm praying. "Please, please let me go to school and be normal for once."

Mom smiles. "I never thought I'd have a child beg to go to school. Okay. Go and be normal. Enjoy getting to know Desi."

"Thank you!" I wrap my arms around her in a tight, fast hug.

Mom laughs, then pushes me back to look into my face, her eyes intense, her mouth tightening. "But if you feel an attack coming on, use your inhaler right away. Don't wait. If this Desi likes you, they'll understand. And call me if you have an attack."

"I will. Promise." I say. I kiss her cheek, grab my backpack, and rush out the door.

Desi's already in the school parking lot leaning against the fence, their face tilted up toward the sun. The hazy morning light makes them look beautiful, almost ethereal. They're wearing a T-shirt that says "My pronouns are not preferred. They're mandatory" written over a trans flag, a plaid shirt open over top. They pull out their ear-buds and walk over to meet me. "Hey."

"Hey." I say back. "Great shirt." Other students watch us—some of the queer kids, and some of the transphobic and homophobic ones, too. Desi is beautiful, in both their soul and their body. I turn my back to the parking lot and watch the cars and bicyclists rush past.

"How's Inez?" I say.

Desi rubs the back of their neck. "Still depressed. But she seemed relieved to talk about it. I told her about you and your visions—there's no way I'd have known, otherwise. She wants to meet you."

"Uh—" I don't know what to say. I didn't expect them to tell anyone. But I didn't tell them to keep it a secret, either. And at least *their* family believes me.

Desi holds up their hand. "Before you say anything, I want you to know..." Their cheeks darken, their jaw clenching. "Inez was raped after her ex posted some nude photos of her online. She got really depressed. Not showering, hardly eating, not doing much of anything." Desi's shoulders slump. "She hasn't left the house at all since it happened, no matter how many times we've offered to walk with her."

"That's awful," I say softly. "I'm so sorry."

Another student walks past, looking at us curiously. Desi takes my arm and leads me along the fence, away from the entrance. "She won't talk to anyone except Nana and me, won't even see a counselor. Her asking to see you—it's the first time she's shown an interest in anything or anybody since...the night it happened."

"Okay. I'll talk with her."

"Today? After school?" Desi asks, insistent.

"Yeah, sure." I push my hair out of my eyes. "I don't know how I can help, but I'll come." I close my eyes. I can't bear for either of them to die.

Desi clears their throat. I wrench my eyes open.

"What's the matter?" Desi asks, frowning.

I swallow tightly. "I had another vision last night. I saw Mason kill my sister." My voice shakes. "He didn't mean to, but that's what he did."

Desi stares at me. "God. Okay. We have to stop him!"

I love that *we*. It makes me feel stronger. "It happens Friday at two forty-five." I take a deep breath. "Jenna still isn't opening up to me, but I'll try again today, after we talk to Inez. And Friday I'll leave school early and go see her, interrupt what happens. I hope that'll change what I saw." It has to.

"You really should call the cops," Desi says, shoving their fingers through their bangs.

My stomach clenches so hard I feel nauseous. "I can't. Besides, they'd never believe me." Well, one might. But at what cost?

Desi huffs their breath. "Fine. But Friday I'm coming with you."

"How'll you get out of class?"

"How will you?" Desi crosses their arms. "Don't worry about me; I'll be there. What time're you leaving?"

"I don't want to go too early, because if I get there before Mason starts hurting her, he could just wait until I'm gone and then end up killing her anyway." I'm talking too fast, but I can't slow down. It's like if I say it fast enough, it won't come true. "But if I can get there just before he...he does it, maybe it'll change things enough so it won't happen."

"You have to try," Desi says. "We both do."

"I'm going to get there by two-thirty, just to be safe. Which means I need to leave at two-fifteen."

"Good," Desi says, standing taller, raising their chin. "I'll be out front waiting. And afterward you can come talk with Inez again. You saw her kill herself that day, too." They wince. "She needs your help just as much."

"Yes," I say. "I promise I'll come."

A motorcycle roars by in the street, drowning out my voice.

"You're lucky, you know," Desi says.

"Lucky?" I stare at them.

"You have the chance to prevent bad things from happening. You got advance warning about your sister, and you gave me that for mine. Now we can work together to save them, instead of being blindsided by their deaths." Desi shudders, like Inez is lying dead in front of them. "If you hadn't told me, if you'd just given up the way you wanted to—" Desi winces. "I don't even want to think about it. It would've destroyed me."

"Me, too," I say softly.

"Right." Desi clenches their fists, raising their chin even higher. "But instead, we're going to save them."

I love their determination, their belief that we can do this. I'm not sure it's true, but they're right; we have to try. It gives me a shot of hope that I won't be doing this alone.

Desi looks down at their worn purple Doc Martens, then back at my face. "I know you haven't had it easy with your visions. But I've always wanted a paranormal ability, like my nana talking to the dead. I'd sit at my nana's feet, listen to her stories of her gift, and ask her when I'd get mine." Desi leans against the fence like their body feels too heavy. "She checked me every time I asked, even talked to the spirits about me, but—" Desi shrugs, looking like they're going to cry. "I'm just like most people. No special talent."

I can taste their disappointment and regret, like damp salt in the air. I wonder what it would've been like to grow up knowing other people had talents like mine, that I wasn't imagining it or mentally ill. Knowing I'd be believed when I talked. I wish my parents were like Desi's nana. Still, to grow up knowing it was possible, seeing it in someone you love, and yet not have that ability? "That must've been hard," I say quietly.

Desi bangs their head back against the fence. "I wanted it so bad. I wanted to be able to talk to my papi. And to other spirits, too, ones who could offer me wisdom or guidance or tell me things I needed to know."

They rub their eyes like they ache from tears they're holding back, the tears I see shimmering there. "I'd be happy with any paranormal talent. And here you have visions, and you're born into a family that doesn't even believe you." They stuff their hands into their jeans, lean further into the fence. "I'm jealous of you. I know it's not cool to admit it, but I am. I wish I had your ability."

I touch their arm. "No, it's fine. I mean—it's better to talk about it than keep it in, you know? And I'm jealous of you, too, of your having your nana to talk to, and that you've always known it was real."

Desi snorts. "Maybe we were born into the wrong families. Our souls went into the wrong bodies."

"Maybe," I say. "I'd give you my visions if I could."

Desi's full mouth turns downward, their eyes still glittering with tears. "It doesn't work like that."

"No, I know. I've tried to wish them away often enough."

"I'm glad it didn't work." Desi swipes at their eyes. "I love my family. I wouldn't trade them for anything. Not even to see the future or talk to the dead." They push off the fence. "I'm just sorry you only seem to get your visions when you have an asthma attack. You need to find another way to see them."

I shrug. "I don't think I can control it."

"There'll be a way; we just have to find it."

"We" again. I smile at them.

"My nana will have some ideas," they say.

I nod, though I doubt it'll help. I've never had a vision without it being triggered by an asthma attack.

"You don't believe me," Desi says intensely. "But trust me—your visions aren't meant to hurt you. My nana always says her ability is a gift from the universe, a kind of blessing."

I can hear how much they believe it; their voice is so strong and sure. And I want to believe them. But it hasn't been my experience. "We'll see," I say.

"Yes, you'll see." They look at me a long moment, their gaze flitting to my lips, then back to my eyes. They lean so close I can smell the mint on their breath.

Are they drawn to me the way I am to them? I lean a little closer, narrowing the space between us. I want to wrap my arms around them, feel their body against mine... Maybe take a risk and kiss them.

Loud laughter sounds out behind us.

Desi pulls back abruptly, blinking.

I don't know if they were feeling the same way or if I was just projecting my feelings onto them. Whatever that moment was, it's gone.

"We're going to help both our sisters," Desi says, pressing my hand between both of theirs like a prayer. "We'll figure it out—and find a way for you to have visions safely—no matter what. I'd do anything for Inez."

Even hang with the sick girl? I envy their closeness. "I want to help my sister, too."

A bus roars by, pumping out exhaust. I turn my head away, trying not to inhale any of it.

"What did Jenna say when you asked her about her husband beating her?" Desi asks after it's quiet again.

"That nothing's happening. I don't know how to get her to open up to me."

"You can't force someone to get help," Desi says, their voice heavy. "But you also can't give up on someone you love."

"I know."

The warning bell rings.

"Listen, we're gonna figure this out. I know it," Desi says, squeezing my arm as we start toward the doors. "And thanks for being willing to come over today."

All through classes I worry about it. I don't know how to help either of our sisters. I don't even know what to say to Inez. I've never thought about suicide, not actively. I've had times I wished I wasn't here, but most of the time I'm desperate to stay alive. What can I say that will help?

11

DESI FINDS ME AT my locker at the end of school. "You ready?"

I slip my books into my bag. "Yeah, I just gotta text my mom, ask her if it's okay," I say, my heart pounding too hard in my chest. I hope Mom gives me permission. I've never had to ask before. But Jenna went out all the time at my age.

Desi invited me to their place to meet their sister, I text. Their gran will be there. Okay?

Dots appear, then disappear, then reappear. Why is she so slow at typing? I chew on my lip as I shut my locker, slide my lock through. Finally my phone pings.

Your breathing okay? Tell me honestly.

Yes. And I have my puffer.

Okay. No more than an hour, then home.

My heart beats fast. "Ready."

"Awesome." Desi grins at me, like they're happy I'm coming, like it's normal for a sixteen-year-old to have to ask permission to stay out after school. Like they believe I can save their sister.

We push out the heavy doors and into the street. "So you and Inez are close?" I say.

"Yeah," Desi says. "Our mamá abandoning us drew us closer; we were the only ones we had left—the two of us and Nana. We tell each other everything. Or we did until Inez's shit boyfriend digitally abused her. All the cyber bullying she got, all the bullying at school, and then her getting raped—" Desi shakes their head. "It really fucked her up. I've tried so hard to be there for her but she shut herself down."

"That's rough," I say.

Desi sniffs. "It's just not like her. Inez needs to talk everything out. Talk and cry and scream. This silence scares me."

It should, since Inez has been seriously thinking of suicide. "I'll talk to her," I say. "We both will."

"Yeah, thanks." Desi smiles at me through their tears.

We walk again in silence. Desi tenses the farther we get from school, their hands clenching and unclenching, their jaw tight.

"You okay?" I say.

"I'm fine," Desi says, stuffing their hands into their pockets.

But they don't look fine. I know they're worried about Inez, scared even.

We walk down streets I don't recognize, Desi leading the way.

"This is our place," Desi says, motioning toward a tall, faded apartment building. We climb up the stairs together to the third floor. Desi holds open the apartment door, the scent of rich stew wafting out. "Nana, I'm home! And I brought Kate."

I follow them into a bright, cramped living room, the walls a sunlight yellow. Plump orange sofas line two walls, taking up most of the space, and plants sit atop almost every surface.

A woman with a deeply lined face, her grey hair tied back, comes into the room, drying her hands on the embroidered-flower apron she wears over her long brown dress. She reaches for both my hands and closes her eyes. I don't know what to do, so I just stand there awkwardly. She opens her eyes again and smiles. "You are welcome here," she says.

She cups my cheek with her warm, papery hand. "Your gift is strong; I can feel it. But it is deeply tied to your heart chakra. It affects your lungs, your heart, and your breathing when you see. No?"

"Yes," I say, blinking.

Desi's grandmother nods. "You must surround yourself with love whenever you see like this. Pull on the love you feel for others and that you know they feel for you. Visualize it like a blanket you wrap around you. That will make it easier for you to breathe."

No one's ever been able to help me like this, never mind believe me. My eyes ache from the tears I'm holding back. "I—thank you so much, Mrs. Flores."

Desi's grandmother laughs, her voice throaty and full. "Call me Nana. Everyone else does. Desi says you have never met another sighted one?"

"You mean someone else with a psychic gift? No. My parents don't believe in it."

"So." Nana nods. "You will come to me any time you have a question. Any time you need to know you are not alone."

Tears burn my eyes. "Thank you," I whisper.

Desi nudges me. "Told you she'd like you," they say.

"After you help my Inez," Nana says, "You come find me, and we talk. We'll see how to get your visions with no stress on your lungs. Okay?"

"Okay," I say.

"Bueno. You see my Inez now?" Nana says, clapping her hands together. "You will help."

"Yes, of course," I say. "I don't know how, though."

"Maybe she will listen to you. She won't listen to an old woman like me."

"Nana, you know that's not true," a frail girl quietly protests as she comes up behind Nana, her face a dull hue compared to her family, her eyes sunken. The baggy black sweatpants and oversized T-shirt she's wearing only emphasize how pale she looks. Dark pouches sag beneath her troubled eyes and her greasy hair hangs limply.

Beside me, Desi exhales sharply.

"I'm Kate," I say.

Inez nods. "Come talk?" She turns away, shuffling down the hall in her slippers. I follow, Desi close behind me. We pass colorful paintings of trees and dancing women, then turn right at an open doorway. As I walk in I'm hit with the stale odor of unwashed body. I blink in the dim light, the blinds pulled down over her windows. The walls are covered with posters of queer painters and their art: Frida Kahlo, Gluck, Amrita Sher-Gil, and Andy Warhol. They overwhelm the small room, making it almost claustrophobic.

Inez slumps onto her bed, her pink, purple, and blue quilt the colours of the bisexual flag. I pull out her desk chair, which almost touches the edge of her bed in the tiny space, and sit.

"So *you're* the girl Desi likes," Inez says, leaning forward.

Desi likes me? My heart beats faster.

"Inez!" Desi says, their face flushing.

Inez smiles at them, though the smile doesn't change the misery in her eyes. "Desi, why don't you let us talk by ourselves?"

They raise their eyebrows at me. I nod.

"Okay." Desi kisses Inez's cheek, then leaves.

"You're Jenna's sister," Inez says slowly.

"Yeah! You know her?"

She shrugs. "We hung out a few times. We weren't really in the same circles. I'm more artsy and queer, and Jenna's—"

"Straight and into sports," I say.

"Exactly." Inez stares at her hands for a long moment, then pats her bi-flag quilt. "My nana sewed this for me," she says. "I'm lucky—she lets me be who I am. Even encourages me. Her and Desi both. It helps that Desi's queer, too."

"That's pretty awesome," I say. "Not everyone has that."

Inez studies me. "Do you?"

"My mom and sister are okay with my being lesbian; my dad tries to ignore it."

"You're lucky you don't like guys," Inez says abruptly.

I hesitate. But the whole school knows what happened. "Because some do shit things like cyber bullying and rape?" I say gently.

"And laugh at your pain, tell you that you deserved it," Inez says bitterly. "Even that you asked for it."

I suck in my breath. "That's horrible," I say. "It wasn't your fault. None of it was your fault."

"Oh, I know," Inez says, hugging herself tightly. "My head knows, anyway. But I can't shake the shame, or how helpless I felt. And all those people telling me it was my fault, that I was a slut because of that nude photo my boyfriend begged me for. Even other girls called me that, and worse."

"That's so wrong," I say. "Victim blaming, siding with the oppressor."

Inez snaps her fingers. "You know it. It's such a fucked up system—patriarchy, white supremacy. Always telling guys to be more macho, less emotional, to sleep with tons of girls to prove their masculinity, but when a girl sleeps with a guy she's slut shamed. It's such a double standard—like girls don't have sexual desire, too."

"It is messed up. It's meant to be; it only benefits cis het white dudes." I feel out of my league. "So—you slept with him?" I say.

"Sure." Inez shrugs, her narrow shoulders all sharp and angled. "Why? You gonna shame me for that, too?"

"No!" I say. "I'm sorry. That was a stupid thing to say. I just—I've never even kissed anyone."

Inez tilts her head, looking at me. "But you know you like girls and nonbinary people."

"Yeah."

"Me, too. I like them all. Girls, boys, nonbinary folks, and gender-nonconforming folks." She sighs, leaning her head back. "And I thought I liked him. I thought he was a good guy. But he's just another misogynist, racist, biphobic asshat. Which shouldn't surprise me. It's what our society is built on." She sounds so hopeless when she says that, like she wants to give up.

"That doesn't mean it can't change," I say. "I see more people waking up to all the oppression around them."

Inez snorts, a strand of her oily hair fluttering.

I don't know what to say to help her, or how it's any different than what Desi or her nana's already told her. I bite my lip. "I know I've only just met you, but I can tell you're someone I'd like to spend time with. I hope I get to know you better."

Inez raises her eyebrows. "Because you like my sibling?"

"No—I like your awareness of the world, of the injustices in it. I like that you're bi; you're part of my community. And I like that you like art." I sweep my hand around to indicate the posters on her walls. "Queer artists. And most of all, I like your openness. Your willingness to talk."

"Sob story and all?" Inez says.

"We've all got trauma," I say. "Different degrees of it, but we all have pain. Talking about it helps us know we're not alone."

Inez rolls her eyes. "You see a shrink or something?"

I shift uneasily. "Actually, I did for a while. It really helped. It might help you, too, to have someone to listen, someone who's not your family." I hesitate. "I can listen, too, but a good therapist can be an amazing support."

"I'll think about it." Inez bows her head, shoulders slumping.

I think of their small apartment, and wonder if money is the issue. I know how lucky I am that my parents could afford to send me to a therapist when I needed one. Good thing I looked it up last night. "There's a guidance counsellor at school you could talk to, and some good helplines like RAINN, and our local rape crisis center. There might be a support group, too."

Inez nods again, sniffing. We sit in quiet for a few seconds, but I can tell she's getting dragged back into her pain.

"Are you going to come back to school?" I ask abruptly, hoping to shake her out of it.

Inez shrugs, still not looking at me, her greasy, stringy hair in her face. "What for?"

"I don't know...to show those misogynists and biphobes that they can't win?"

Inez jerks her head up and stares at me, her eyes so full of pain I want to look away. A faint smile crosses her lips. "That's the best reason I've heard." She swallows. "Desi said you saw me killing myself."

"Uh—yeah." I shift awkwardly on the hard chair. "I had to tell them. They want to help. I do, too."

"Because you don't think I should die."

"No, you can't! Desi and Nana—they'd be devastated. They'd never get over it."

"I know," Inez whispers. "I don't want to hurt them. But sometimes the pain is so bad I don't think I can get through it."

"That sounds pretty unbearable." I want to take away her hurt but I don't know how. "I can't imagine the kind of pain you're in."

Inez smiles through her tears. "You have pain, too. I can see it."

"It's nothing," I shake my head.

"Pain is pain. It all hurts. So tell me about yours."

"I'm just—out sick a lot. With asthma." My voice falters. Inez is serious about killing herself. My troubles sound so little in comparison. What can I say to change her mind? "Asthma is so common it doesn't sound like anything, but I have it really bad. I never stop thinking about how quickly I can go from being okay to having a really bad attack—and maybe dying."

Inez shivers. "That's scary." She looks away.

"It is." I bite my lip so hard it hurts. I don't know if I should say what's in my head or not.

12

Inez lifts her head when I hesitate. "Whatever it is, just say it."

"Okay." I lick my dry lips. "I think about dying a lot. Every time I have an attack, I feel like I'm being strangled. Sometimes I have to fight to live. But I never want to give up. Especially when I'm scared I'll die."

Inez's eyes glisten. She pushes the oily hair out of her eyes. "I don't want to give up, either—at least not most of the time. When some of the kids at school sent me death threats, it just made me want to fight harder. But after I was raped, all the fight went out of me."

"That never should've happened to you," I say. "I know you're really hurting, but you can't give up, okay?" I shift on the hard chair, the wood creaking. "I've almost died a few times, and besides the terror what I remember most was how upset my family was. How fragile they looked. Like a gust of wind could flatten them."

Inez doesn't say anything; she just nods at me to go on. I lick my lips and keep talking. "I know your pain is bad; worse than I can imagine. But you have the chance to live—to show those asshats that you're not going to let them get the better of you. You have the chance to be happy. To do things that make you feel alive." My voice breaks. "And maybe even help others who've been through the same things to know that they're not alone. That it wasn't their fault, either."

Inez swipes at her cheeks. "I guess," she whispers.

I rub my sore lips. "There was a girl in the hospital with me who had asthma, too. She died when she was ten. I think of her every day. It could've been me." My voice shakes. I've never said that to anyone before. "So I try to do what makes me happy. I want to make a positive difference for others, and spend time with the people I love. The people who are here with me now."

"Thank you," Inez says hoarsely, looking down at her bed.

I don't know if I've helped her or not. I wish I knew what to say. I think of my vision of her, the first one, where she was holding the photo of her mom, Desi, and her. I grip my hands together. "Your mom leaving hurt you. It probably left a really big hole," I say.

Inez raises one eyebrow, then nods.

"I know she didn't die, but she still disappeared out of your life." I dig my nails into my flesh. "Think how bad it hurt you, what a loss it was, and how much worse it'll be for Desi and your nana if you die—especially if you die at your own hands. They'll never get over it."

There's a flare of emotion in Inez's eyes. Anger? I hope I didn't say the wrong thing. But my seeing her mom's photo in my vision must be important.

"Your mom abandoned you all," I say, my hands trembling. "If you kill yourself, you're abandoning them, too. And they need you."

Inez's eyes brighten. Definitely anger. And something else.

I swallow tightly. "You die, and they've been abandoned twice. Only the hole you'll rip in them will be so much bigger."

Inez pushes off her bed, her mouth tight. I'm scared she's going to throw me out, but she walks over to her desk and picks up a picture frame that was lying face down.

She brings it over. "This is the woman who wasn't strong enough to stay, to love her kids and her mom," she says tightly. "Who didn't care about the hole she made in us, the grief she caused." She tosses the picture frame back onto her desk and straightens. "I'll never be like her. Never!"

"Good," I say. I hesitate. "So—you'll stay?"

Inez throws back her head and laughs. "You're as stubborn as Desi! You're made for each other."

My ears burn.

Inez crouches down in front of me. "Yes, I'll try to stay. For the people I love."

"I'm glad. They really do need you."

Inez leans over and squeezes my hand. "I knew you were a good one when Desi started talking about you. I'm glad you came."

My body relaxes a little. "You're a good one, too. I hope that you'll stay," I say. "Desi loves you so much. So does your nana. And I think we could be friends."

"I think so, too," Inez says, standing.

"Thank you." I get up and hug her fast. "I'll give you my number if you ever want to talk."

Inez grabs her phone and types in the numbers I rattle off. "Thanks," she says quietly.

I walk out of her room—and bump into Desi. They grab me and blush. They must've been standing there listening the whole time.

"You wanna talk to Nana now?" they say.

I check my cell. "I wish I could, but I've got to get home. Another time?"

"You got it," they say. "Come on. I'll walk you."

"Let me just call Jenna first." I tap Jenna's number, and it rings and rings but she doesn't answer.

I slap my forehead. "She's at the bakery today. Lemme just text her." **Jenna—any time you want to talk I'm here. Would love to get together tomorrow.**

I wait, but she doesn't text back. "Okay, let's go."

Outside, the sky is a bright, clear blue and the sun is warm on my skin. We walk in silence for a block, passing people walking their dogs or coming home with groceries, old men smoking, and kids carrying instrument cases or sports bags. Cars drive past in both directions at a steady pace as rush hour starts.

Desi touches my arm. "Thanks for speaking so honestly with Inez. You were amazing; I think it'll help."

I knew they'd listened! "I hope so," I say. "I like her."

"Yeah, Inez is a sweetheart. She'd never hurt anyone intentionally, and always tries to help others."

They could be describing themselves.

Desi rubs the back of their neck. "She used to be so upbeat before her ex posted her photo online, and that bastard assaulted her, and the school became a cesspool of malicious gossip and threats. It's a good sign she talked with you. She doesn't seem to care about much anymore."

"She cares about you and Nana."

"Yeah. Listen," they say, gesturing widely with their arm, almost hitting my head, "Sorry! Uh, do you want to hang out sometime? I mean, when we're not trying to save one of our sisters? Like, a date?"

My heart speeds up so fast I get breathless. "Yeah! I'd love to."

Desi's solemn face breaks into a smile. "Great! That's great. I wasn't sure—"

"I wasn't sure, either."

Desi stops walking to stare at me. "But I've tried to show you I like you so many times."

"You have? When?" I ask, my breath hitching.

"When I offered to carry your backpack. When I'd hold the door open for you, or offer you a stick of gum."

"I thought you were just being nice to the sick kid. You're so kind to everyone." I didn't think they could like me that way. I underestimated them.

"Being nice?" Desi scratches their head. "I try to be a good person—but Kate, that was me being interested in you. For months."

They look so dumbfounded I laugh. "I guess you have to be a little less subtle with me."

"Less subtle. Got it," Desi says. Then they lean in to kiss me.

Their lips are soft and gentle as they slide across mine. My whole body tingles.

Desi pulls away to look at me. I tug them back, and kiss them again. It feels so good—better than I can remember anything ever feeling.

I have to pull away to catch my breath. "Wow."

"Wow?" Desi lightly smooths their thumb against my hot cheek.

"Wow." I grin at them. "But wait—how could you not know I liked you?"

"What should I have seen?" Desi asks, smiling.

"Me staring at you all the time. Me trying to be near you, like running on the track with you and setting off an attack. Or hovering near your locker."

"I thought you were just aware of another queer kid. Queer-dar."

"I see I'm going to have to be a lot less subtle with you, too," I say, grinning.

Desi laughs and grabs my hand, swinging it as we walk, the sun warm on our backs. "You never seemed to make a move. Other queer kids flirt with me, give me their number, touch me."

"I don't flirt," I say dryly. "I don't think I know how."

"I know. That's one of the things I like about you."

"No flirting. Got it."

"Hey, just be yourself. I like who you are, Kate."

"I like who you are, too," I say. I feel so light I think I could fly.

We turn the corner onto my street. "My house is just up there—fifth one on the right," I say, pointing at our narrow two-story brick house, the front door painted a sky blue.

Desi whistles. "Nice place," they say, and I know they're thinking of their family's small apartment.

"Your place felt homey and warm," I say.

"Yeah, it's the people in it that really matter." Desi leans forward and kisses me again, and it feels just as good as it did last time.

I pull away reluctantly. I don't want to go—but I don't want Mom to look down the street and see us kissing.

Desi squeezes my hand. "Let me know how your sister is. If we have to go talk to her, we will."

"I promise. And you do the same. Though if I get another vision I might know first."

MOM'S WAITING FOR ME at the door. She leans in close, and I know she's listening for a wheeze. "You have a good time?"

I can't explain it to her; she'd probably freak. "Yeah. Thanks."

Mom pushes my hair out of my eyes. "That Desi I saw walking you up the street?"

My face burns. "Yeah."

Mom smiles, but it looks a little odd. "Good."

"They're kind, Mom! And they were just making sure I got home safe."

"I'm sure they were. Just don't grow up too fast."

"I'm sixteen! Jenna was going out all the time at my age."

"I know," Mom says, her eyes watering.

Uh oh. Maybe I shouldn't have mentioned that. "I'm not Jenna," I say softly. "I'm not going to elope." Mom nods again. "I know." She squeezes me in a quick hug and lets me go.

"I've got homework," I say, and walk up to my room.

I don't know what to say to Jenna to get through to her, but I have to try something different. She should be home by now. I video call her.

"You look serious," she says when she picks up. "You okay?"

"I'm fine," I say. "I just—I wanted to say that I love you. And any time you want to talk about anything, no matter what, I'm here."

Jenna squints at me through the screen, the dark smears below her eyes making her look vulnerable and weary. "You still think Mason's hurting me? Because I told you, you're wrong. He's my prince. You've seen how thoughtful he is, bringing me things he knows I like."

How do I break through her denial? I think back to the article I skimmed last night. I shouldn't push her, not while she's defensive; it'll only make her defend him more. I clench my phone. "Yeah—he can be very thoughtful."

She nods sharply. "Damned right."

"I'm just saying—we all have hard times, right? So I'm here, and so are Dad and Mom, any time you want to lean on us."

Jenna snorts. "What would I need to lean on you for?" Her lips curl. "You're the one who's always sick and helpless, needing everyone else to help you."

I grit my teeth, biting back the things I shouldn't say, the hurt and anger. I go over what she said. Does she think I'm saying she's weak? "I know you're strong and independent. But even the strongest of us need to talk sometimes. That's all I'm saying."

Jenna's face relaxes. "I'm good. But thanks." She squints at the screen again. "I need to get supper ready. Talk to you soon, Kate." She ends the call.

I want to scream. Nothing I'm doing is getting through to her—and there's only three days until Friday.

I wake up feeling better than usual—I didn't even cough in the night. I have a quick shower, then go downstairs to do my peak flow levels. Green.

I show Mom triumphantly, and she doesn't even try to keep me home. I rush through breakfast and get to school early.

Desi's in the schoolyard, leaning against the wall, laughing at something someone said. Just hearing them laugh makes me happier. They turn and see me, like they could feel me watching them, and stride over. Their T-shirt says "What a beautiful day to respect other people's pronouns." It makes me grin. "Hey."

"Hey," I say, my heart fluttering in my chest. "How's Inez?"

Desi runs their fingers through their bangs. "Better-ish. Talking to us more. Coming out of her room more."

"That sounds—hopeful," I say.

Desi laughs, their voice rich and full. "You sound surprised."

I kick at the asphalt. "I told you—I've never been able to protect anyone before."

"And I told you it'll be different this time." Desi nudges me. "How's Jenna?"

"Still not admitting Mason's hurting her."

"You gotta be patient with her."

"But I only have until Friday," I say. "I don't know how to get through to her."

Desi sucks in their bottom lip thoughtfully, looking cute. "What do you think she needs?"

"I don't know!" I say.

"Maybe she doesn't, either. Wanna brainstorm over lunch?"

I do. But in the cafeteria where people will make rude comments or asthma jokes? I don't want Desi to see me like that. But they must have it before. I shuffle my feet.

"What's wrong?"

"Noth—" I start to say, but they level their gaze at me and I know I won't get away with it. I sigh. "I don't want you to see me the way others do."

Desi raises one eyebrow. "Smart? Kind? Cute?" They lean closer and whisper, "Gifted?"

"No—sick."

They crinkle their forehead. "Your asthma's not a secret."

"Neither is the way the others hate me for it."

Their eyes flash. "Hate how?"

So they don't know. I shrug, my face hot. "Pretend I'm the new kid. Call me Wheezy Face or other crap. Tell me how much they hate me for the no-scent policy the school put in place. Ignore me."

Desi clenches their fists. "Who?"

I shrug again. "It's a lot of them." *Though Gabby's the worst.*

"Shit, Kate, I had no idea. I'm sorry." Their face is flushed darker, their eyes too bright, like they're going to cry.

"Hey, it's okay," I say, touching their arm.

"No, it's not."

And they're right. It isn't.

"Is it anyone from my friend group, any of the queer kids?"

"No," I say.

"If you tell me who it is, I'll talk to them," Desi says, "Help them see they're being poop rags."

I take a step back. "No!"

"You sure?"

"It won't do anything. I mean—people like you, so they'll go along with what you say while you're there, but when they catch me alone—"

"It'll be worse," Desi says slowly.

I bow my head, my chest hot.

"Hey." Desi lifts my chin with their finger. "You know they're bottom feeders to treat you that way, right? There isn't anything wrong with you."

"Thanks," I whisper, willing the tears in my eyes to evaporate.

"And you've got something most of them don't. You've got a gift."

"I'm trying to see it that way, instead of a curse," I say.

Desi pulls me into a hug. "I told you; we're gonna change what happens with your visions—together."

I lean into them, breathing in the soapy clean scent of their skin, the peppermint lip balm they're wearing. Their arms are strong around me, their body soft in the right places. I wish we could stay like this forever, in our own little bubble.

Desi pulls back, looking into my face. "So—lunch?"

I nod, hoping I won't regret it.

The cafeteria is loud—teens laughing, yelling, talking, burping, slapping tables or hands, stomping feet, pounding out rhythms.

I want to shrink back around the door, but Desi's already seen me and is waving. They must've been watching the entrance.

I force myself over to their table—the cool queer kids table, with lots of stylish haircuts and brightly dyed hair, creative makeup and painted fingernails, layered or bright clothing, and little flashes of pride flags on shoelaces, belts, bracelets, piercings, and shirts.

Desi waves me to the seat beside them, then introduces me.

"I love your rainbow glasses!" one of the kids says, grinning.

"Yeah, shove it in their faces!" another says.

"I love your nonbinary pin," I say.

They dip their chin in response, grinning, and just like that the others all seem to accept me. Yet I can't relax my shoulders or draw in a full breath.

I unpack my lunch—a cheese-and-lettuce sandwich, applesauce, carrot and celery sticks, and juice. Plain and "healthy." Laughter and conversation flies around me.

Desi leans in close. "I'm glad you came." They smile at me, their brown eyes warm.

I smile back, my shoulders loosening. "Me, too."

"So, you wanna brainstorm?"

I bite into my sandwich, nodding.

"What've you done so far, and what's her response been?" Desi asks, spooning up their orange rice. I can smell the tomato and spices—so much more appetizing than my sandwich.

I swallow fast, then catch them up.

Desi frowns. "It sounds like she's both in denial and being defensive."

"Yep." I take another bite of my sandwich.

Desi sips from their thermos. "And you're careful to talk to her when you know he's not around?"

"Yeah—she'd never listen to me if he was there. And I know it could make the abuse worse. He's never there during the day, not until about six-thirty."

Desi twirls their spoon between their fingers. "So what's different about this Friday? Why is he home so early? And how do we keep him away?"

I sit up straighter. "I never thought about preventing him from being there! I'd only thought about needing to stop him." I take a gulp of water. "Maybe I could call in a car repair job at his work and say it has to be him, at two-thirty Friday, so he won't be anywhere near Jenna around the time when he killed her."

"I like it," Desi says, pointing their spoon at me and smiling. "Just be sure to use someone else's phone—you can use mine—and disguise your voice. Or better yet, send an email from a fake email account."

"But what if he says he can't do it then?"

Desi shrugs. "We make it super enticing, and say you're only in town at that time." They stir their rice. "He's a mechanic, so he's really into cars, yeah?"

"Yes."

"He have a favorite?"

"He's always talking about an Audi R Eight. And I know he's got some spare parts just in case."

Desi wags their spoon at me. "There you go."

I pick up my sandwich. "But how do I convince him it's real?"

"We'll swipe some pics from the net, and look up how cis het guys talk about them." Desi taps their cell phone, then shows me the screen. "Let's write the email!" They log onto an anonymous email site and we write the email together, attaching a pic of an Audi R8.

"Thank you!" I say. "You're a genius!"

Desi laughs. "You came up with it."

"Yeah, but I wouldn't have thought of it if you hadn't suggested keeping him away."

"We make a good team," Desi says, nudging my thigh with theirs.

I grin. For the first time I actually feel hopeful about being able to protect Jenna.

"Desi's good at almost anything they jump into," one of the queer kids says, leaning towards us.

I stiffen. I've been so focused on Desi and on protecting Jenna that I forgot the other kids were there. "Uh—what we were talking about, it's confidential, okay?"

The kid who spoke to me holds up their hands. "I'd never tell. None of us here would. We gotta stick together."

"Thanks, Raphael," Desi says, smiling.

Desi's phone pings. I lean over. "Is that—?"

"Yep!" Desi cackles, opening the email. "We got him—hook, line, and sinker!" They raise their hand for a high five.

I slap it. Maybe we'll be able to save Jenna, after all.

14

DESI AND I WALK into English together, our shoulders touching. Even after Desi's seated across from me, the glow doesn't go away.

"You gonna elope, Wheezy Breath?" Gabby asks, leaning toward me.

I stiffen but don't respond, don't even look at her.

All through Ms. Hirano's lesson I keep peeking over at Desi even though I tell myself not to. They like me back! They're helping me protect Jenna, they don't see me as some victim because other kids bully me, and they invited me to sit with their friends. I almost don't believe it's happening.

Unless...it isn't? They might only be hanging with me so I'll help them save their sister. What if we can't save Inez, what then? I sneak a look at them, then another, but they're absorbed in their own thoughts.

My lungs feel thick, like thousands of tiny tentacles are spreading through them in a web, making me struggle for air. And what if we can't save Jenna? No, I can't go there. I cough, clenching my hands.

I won't have another asthma attack in front of Desi, in front of the whole class. I prime my puffer and inhale as deeply as I can. I cough harder.

"Okay, Kate?" Ms. Hirano asks, uncrossing her legs.

I wish she wouldn't draw attention to me. "Okay!" I say hoarsely.

Desi swivels around in their chair, their eyes worried. Others stare at me, too.

"Wheezy face," Gabby hisses.

"Gabby, did you have something to say?" Ms. Hirano asks, raising one perfectly shaped, arched eyebrow.

"No, Ma'am," Gabby says, her cheeks flushing dark.

I inhale from my puffer again as quietly as I can, but it's not a quiet thing.

Ms. Hirano waves her hand at the class. "I'd like each of you to pick one recently banned book that is not banned in our district, read it, and write an essay on why you disagree or agree with the ban." She looks up at the clock. "Class dismissed. Kate, would you hang back for a minute?"

The others rush out. I gather my stuff and walk up to Ms. Hirano's desk. "You wanted to see me?"

Ms. Hirano smiles. "It's great to see you back in class, and lovely to hear you speak up the way you did the other day."

My chest prickles. I didn't speak up at all today. I was too busy daydreaming about Desi and worrying about Jenna and Inez. "Thank you."

Ms. Hirano tucks her hair behind her ear, her bracelets jangling. "But you've been looking a little stressed. Want to talk about it?"

"I'm not going to elope like my sister," I say.

Ms. Hirano laughs. When I don't she straightens, the laughter leaving her face. "Oh. You're serious. Has someone suggested that?"

I nod reluctantly. "A few students." Especially Gabby.

"We should never be judged by our family's actions, only by our own."

I kick at the worn linoleum floor. "I agree—but that's not usually how it works."

Ms. Hirano hums a note under her breath, then looks at me levelly. "I don't usually tell students this, but I think you can keep things to yourself, can't you?"

I nod, wondering where she's going.

"When I was a teen and first coming into all my glorious transness," Ms. Hirano says, gesturing at herself, "My father, who was a tremendous transphobe and homophobe, vandalized my local queer community center which had supported me. I was so angry and ashamed that I didn't want to show my face—but I did. Most of the community rallied around me; our community is like that. The ones who didn't, who blamed me for my father's actions?" She leans closer. "They weren't people I liked or had respect for, anyway."

I nod. She's right about that.

"The same goes for anyone who puts you down or acts like they're better than you. They don't deserve your energy."

So she did hear Gabby. "That's true."

Ms. Hirano taps the top of my head. "I want to see you holding your head up high, girl! Be proud of who you are, all the challenges you've overcome, the biases and isms you've endured. It's part of what makes you strong, stronger than the Gabbys in this world."

Wow. I stare at her. "Thank you."

"And if you're worried about whether a certain individual likes you," she says, her brown eyes sparkling, "I think you'll find they're just as entranced with you as you are with them."

My cheeks prickle with heat like a sunburn. I wish I could fly out of the room. "I—yeah. Thanks."

Ms. Hirano pats my shoulder. "Trust yourself, Kate—I think you've got a pretty good sense of people." Students start entering the room. "Dang. I meant to give you more space to talk. Do you want to come by after school?"

"Uh—not today," I say. "I'm meeting up with someone. Another time?"

"Any time," Ms. Hirano says. She leans across her desk, grabs a pass, and scribbles her signature. "I promise next time I'll be a better listener."

"No—what you said was perfect," I say. And it was.

Desi's leaning against my locker after school. They push off when they see me, smiling broadly. "You never got your talk with Nana. I told her about you only having visions when you have an asthma attack," Desi says, leaning in so close they could kiss me. "And she thinks she can help. Wanna come over now?"

"Sure," I say. "Just let me text my mom." I hope she'll let me. But two days in row?

Going over to Desi's to study, their gran and sister there. Okay?

How's your breathing?

Good, no wheeze, and I have my puffer. Promise I'll call if my asthma acts up. Please? I need this normalcy.

Dots come up on the screen, disappear, then come up again. She's probably deleting half of what she's writing. I want to scream at her to hurry up.

Desi glances at me. "Okay?"

I sigh. "I hope so. My mom's a bit overprotective."

The dots turn into text. **Okay. One hour, then home.**

I grin. "I have an hour!"

"Awesome," Desi says. "Let's make it count."

"Come, sit," Nana says, waving toward the scarred wood kitchen table. I sit on a solid wood chair, Desi across from me, grinning lopsidedly while Nana carries a teapot over, setting it onto a hotplate beside three mugs, a jar of honey, and two spoons. She's wearing the same embroidered apron over a lavender dress.

Nana eases herself into a chair to the left of me, then reaches out her wrinkled hands, palm up. I take her hands; they're soft and papery, yet strong. "Bueno. Solo un momento."

I nod.

Nana closes her eyes, breathing slowly and deeply. The lines in her face are etched deep, making her kindness more visible, her skin a darker bronze than Desi's. I can tell she's both laughed and cried a lot in her life.

Desi shifts in their chair but I don't look their way; I don't want to interrupt whatever's happening.

Nana's hands tighten on mine, then she opens her eyes and lets go. "You have much fear, yes? About your visions? And doubt. You must let it go, as much as you can." She shakes her head. "It blocks your heart chakra, makes it harder for your visions to come without pulling hard on that chakra. And you must draw on love."

I bow my head. "It's hard not to be afraid when I see people in trouble and I can't help them."

Nana pats my hand. "You would not be given these visions if you could not help."

Which is what Desi said, and I've been clinging desperately to it, even though I don't really believe it. My eyes burn, my vision blurring. "But I couldn't. I didn't protect any of them—" My chest tightens, and I force myself to breathe slower. "I tried."

Nana frowns, tilting her head. "You warned them?"

"Yeah, I tried to."

"And they did not listen?"

"They didn't believe me," I say. "Not even my parents. They all thought I was lying or trying to get attention, or there was something wrong with my brain."

"Ah." Nana sits back. "That is a problem; their doubt crept into you. You must let it go."

"How?" I ask.

"You know your visions have turned out true, yes? Go over them, see them, believe in your gift. And see yourself with love."

Pain clenches my heart, and I wince. I don't want to think about all the people I couldn't protect.

Desi leans forward and touches my hand, like they can sense my pain.

"If that is too hard," Nana says, "You think of new visions. You were right about Inez. You were right about your sister."

Of course Desi told her. "Okay."

"You must do this often," Nana says. "Believe in your gift. Shed your doubt and fear. Now you have help." She waves at Desi. "You have us who believe you; it will all turn out different. You will see."

I nod again, but I don't really believe it. I hope for it—but I don't know if we'll be able to.

Nana sighs, tapping her fingertips against the wood table. "It is important. You want your visions without the struggle to breathe, you must trust yourself and release your fear and doubt. You must work on this every day. And draw love to you—your love for others, the love they have for you. Understand?"

"Yes," I say. "Thank you."

She keeps tapping, her knuckles swollen with arthritis. "And you must meditate; this will strengthen your gift, help clear the blockage. You stare at one spot or you close your eyes, quiet your mind. Thoughts come, you let them go. Tell them 'Later.' You do this every day, too. You do these both, you make it easier for visions to come, easier to breathe. Okay?"

"Yes," I say. "Thank you so much." I actually have something I can work on now. Something that might help.

Nana smiles, the wrinkles in her face deepening, especially around her kind eyes and mouth. "Bueno. Now you drink this tea." She pours tea into the three mugs, her arms shaking slightly, and hands us each a mug. "If you like, I give you some to take home. It is manzailla. Good for calm."

"You might know it as chamomile," Desi says.

I take a cautious sip. It has a flowery, faintly sweet taste to it, and a slightly bitter aftertaste.

"You no like, you add honey," Nana says, gesturing to the jar.

I glance at Desi. They grin, grab the jar of honey and a spoon, and scoop some into their mug, stirring. "It can taste bitter if you're not use to it, or if you like sweets. Want some?"

"Yes please," I say.

They grab the other spoon, scoop up a generous dollop of honey, and stir it into my tea. "Try it now."

I take another cautious sip. The sweetness is soothing, and so is the flowery taste.

Nana cackles. "You have a sweet tooth like my Desi!"

My face grows hot. "I do."

"You are good for each other." Nana sips her tea, her eyes twinkling above her mug.

"Nana!" Desi says, groaning, clapping their cheeks.

My face burns hotter, but inside I want to laugh. I take another sip of tea to hide my smile.

My cell buzzes. "I've got to get home soon," I say reluctantly. "I promised."

Nana nods. "It's good you respect your mamá. She worries about you."

I glance at Desi.

Desi shakes their head. "I didn't tell her anything!"

"The spirits," Nana says. "They tell me your mamá almost lost you a few times to this asthma. All the more reason you need to practice what I taught you."

"I will," I say.

Nana stands, grabs another mug from the cupboard and pours some tea. She sits back down. "You are lucky your gift warned you about your sister. It doesn't always about our loved ones."

"It doesn't?" I say.

Nana shakes her head. "Especially not when we worry about them too much." She glances at the mug she just poured.

Inez walks in. It's uncanny how Nana knew.

"Hey," Inez says. She looks better than she did yesterday; her hair is washed, and while she's still wearing sweats and a baggy T-shirt they look clean.

"How're you feeling?" I say.

"A bit better," Inez says, running her hands through her clean hair. "Thanks for the talk yesterday."

"Any time," I say. "I mean it."

Desi stands, pulling Inez into a hug. "I'm glad you showered. That's a step towards feeling better."

Inez snorts and pulls back.

"Your tea, mija," Nana says, pointing.

Inez kisses Nana on her cheek. "Thank you." She picks up the mug and sits in Desi's empty chair.

Desi grabs my backpack off the floor. "You ready?"

"Yeah. Thank you again, Mrs...Nana," I say. "Inez, sorry I have to go, but my mom is kinda strict." She looks so much better already, maybe she's ready for another step. "Want to walk back with us?"

Inez shrinks in her seat. "Not today," she says. "Maybe another time."

Desi and Nana glance at each other, their eyes troubled.

"Okay," I say easily, hoping I didn't push her too hard. "Whenever you're ready."

Inez lifts her head. "I will be. Just not yet."

15

DESI WALKS WITH ME, their stride matching mine.

"Thanks for getting your nana to talk with me," I tell them. "She seems really nice. I wish I'd been able to talk to her years ago."

Desi's face brightens. "I'm glad you liked her. She's been doing this for a really long time; she knows what she's talking about." Desi's steps slow. "It's important to figure out how to work with your gift. Not everyone can."

Their voice sounds heavy and brittle, like they're talking from pain. I think of Inez crumpling the photo. "Your mom?"

"Yeah." Desi shoves their hands into their pockets. "She could talk to the spirits, like Nana. Only she got caught up with people who told her it wasn't real, that it was all in her head, that Nana was just a superstitious old woman—and she started thinking that she had schizophrenia or something."

Desi jerks their hand up to wipe at their eyes. "I was real little then, but I heard some of the arguments she and Nana used to have. I think mamá left us because she couldn't handle the truth, couldn't handle her gift."

"I'm sorry," I say, touching their arm.

"Me, too. I miss her. I know Inez and Nana do even more. They remember her better." Desi looks at me, their eyes glossy with tears. "I'm glad you learned something from Nana, glad she could help. I want you healthy when you have a vision, not trying to cough up a lung."

I snort. "Me, too."

"But it was also good for Nana to have someone need her that way again, for her to have someone to guide in the ways of the gift. We'll have to have you over a lot more often."

So I can learn from Nana. "That's great," I say quietly.

"What?" Desi says, turning to me. "Don't you want to?"

"No, I do, I just—" I bite my lip. Will they think I'm too needy?

"What?" Desi frowns. "Out with it."

My chest is too tight. "I hope you want me there for me, too."

Desi stares at me, then laughs. "Of course I do, you goof!" They wrap their arm around my shoulders, draw me to them, and kiss the top of my head before letting me go. "That's the main reason. I like you; I want you around. But if Nana can help things get easier for you, and it helps her at the same time, well that makes me even happier. Two people I care about doing better."

My body relaxes, my chest loosening up. "I'm glad."

We walk in silence for a while, the sound of the cars in the road loud. Desi's footsteps grow heavier and slower. I wonder if they're thinking of their mother again.

"Do you ever hear from your mom?" I say. "Do you know where she is?"

"No to both questions," Desi says, their hands becoming fists. "It burns me up. Inez really needs her right now, and she can't even be bothered to text us." Desi blows out their breath hard. "I know she couldn't handle having the gift, or Nana having it—but she doesn't have to worry about that with us; neither Inez or I have the gift, even though I'd give anything to have it. If I could take hers I would, relieve her of what she sees as a burden. But she doesn't know any of that. She doesn't even know me." Their voice breaks.

"She's missing out on so much," I say. "You're fantastic, one of the best people I know. Inez, too."

Desi kicks at a flattened soda can. "Thanks. She barely got to know us before she took off. If I ever have kids I'll never abandon them, or fail to show an interest in them, or let my own problems become bigger than them."

"I believe it," I say. "If you have kids you'll be a great parent. You help so many people already."

Desi's tight face eases into a smile. "Thanks, mi Cielito."

I raise my eyebrows at them.

"My little sky," they say.

I laugh. I've never been called that in my life, but somehow I like it from Desi.

Desi slips their hand into mine. "I think I'm falling for you. Hard."

My heart flutters like a moth in my chest. "That's good, because I already have for you."

They stop right there on the sidewalk, people passing us by, and pull me to them, kissing me. I lose myself in the kiss, in the softness of their lips, the hitch of their breath, the spicy sweetness of their scent, the way their hands cup my cheeks, holding me steady, anchoring me to them. There's just the two of us, the now, their lips insistent on mine.

When they pull away I stumble. They catch my arm, grinning. "Kissing you feels so good."

"It does," I say dazedly. Everything felt so right when we were kissing. I want to kiss them again, to go on kissing them.

A car horn blares loudly, clearing my head. "My mom'll be worried if I'm late. Maybe angry, try to ground me. And I want to be able to keep spending time with you."

"You're right. Let's get going."

We start walking again. I reach for their hand, the warmth of their skin pressing into mine, like it's sinking into my heart.

I wish their mother had never wounded them by abandoning them. Wish I could ease their old pain. I know I can't change it, but I can give them my truth now. "I feel happier with you," I say. "Like everything is better when I'm around you."

"I do with you, too," Desi says.

"You do?"

Desi squeezes my hand. "Of course."

"Even though I might fail?"

"That's got nothing to do with why I like you," Desi says earnestly. "And Nana'll help you make it easier for you. I told you; it's gonna be different this time."

I love their faith in their nana, in themself, and in me. "You're right," I say softly. "I'm sorry I keep needing reassurance. It's been so hard seeing people in danger and not be able to protect them."

Desi stops. "It must've been hell. But it's different now. And you don't have to apologize. I'd have felt the same way if I'd been in your shoes, without support."

I love how easily they empathize.

"So I'll reassure you as many times as you need until you see things are gonna be different."

We don't have long to wait. Friday's almost here.

16

MOM'S WAITING FOR ME when I get home, leaning in to not so subtly check my breathing. "How's your asthma been?" Mom says.

"Fine," I say. "I would've told you if I'd had an attack." Or a teacher would've. I dump my backpack on the floor and head into the kitchen, grabbing an apple.

Mom follows me. "Have you checked your peak flow?"

She knows I haven't; I only just got home. And she didn't even ask me about Desi or my day. It's like she's my doctor, not my mom. I bite into the apple, chewing.

"Kate, I asked you a question," Mom says, her voice sharp.

I swallow so fast I almost choke on the apple chunk. "Can't you ever talk to me about anything else?" I shout.

Mom takes a step back. "What do you mean?"

"It's like our entire relationship is about my being sick," I say, gripping the apple so hard my fingers ache.

Mom sets her hands on her hips. "Well, if you'd take better care of your health—"

"No!" I shout. "I'm doing okay, not even a wheeze, but the only thing you can ask me about is my breathing and peak flow readings! Why can't we ever talk about anything else?"

Mom shakes her head. "Deep breaths, please. You don't want to set yourself off."

"See?" I scream, tears blurring my vision.

Mom takes a deep breath, like she can take one for me, and walks over to the coffee maker, pouring herself a mug full. She turns back around, leaning against the counter. "Okay. What do you want to talk about?"

"Anything!" I say. "Books I'm reading, our day, what's happening in society. That I'm queer in a homophobic world. That I have a new joyfriend. Or how about how worried I am about Jenna? Anything but how my breathing is."

Mom turns her mug around in her hands. "You need me to monitor you."

"Yeah, I did when I was a kid."

Mom nods, her lips pressed so tightly together they almost disappear, her eyes watering.

I scrape out a chair and sit at the kitchen table. "I do need you, Mom," I say. "But I can take care of my asthma most of the time. I'll let you know when I can't."

Mom sits beside me, setting her mug down, and sniffs. "I'm sorry if I've been too focused on your health. It's just..." Her hands tremble. She grabs her mug with both hands, and takes a deep breath. "I lost my mom, your grandma, to an asthma attack. I don't want to lose you, too."

I stare at her. She doesn't talk about her mom much. "You never told me that."

"I didn't want to scare you."

I sit back. "How old was your mom when she—?"

Mom's shoulders curve inward. "She was only thirty-five. It happened when I was ten."

I knew her mom had died when she was young, but not that young. "That must've been so hard," I say.

Mom wipes at a tear sliding down her cheek. "I was with her when she died," she says. "I got her inhaler, called nine-one-one, but she still died. I know now that it wasn't my fault but I always felt that if

I'd just been a little quicker in noticing her symptoms, in getting her inhaler—" She rubs her eyes, her lips trembling.

"God, Mom," I say. "It wasn't your fault. And you were just a kid." I squeeze her arm. "You shouldn't have had to witness that." No wonder she hovers over me so much. It makes me ache for the scared, grieving kid she was.

I get up and hug her, and Mom clings to me for a moment, then lets me go. I sink back down into my chair.

Mom smiles a watery smile at me. "Thank you. I feel better now that I've told you that. I'll try to be more chill."

I clasp my hands in my lap. "That'd help. And...I need you to know me, beyond my asthma."

Mom sniffs. "I do know you."

"You know my health." I rub my hands on my jeans. "But do you know what I like?"

"You like Desi," Mom says with a smile.

"Well, yeah. That's who. What else?"

"Um—books?"

"Yeah. And graphic novels, making crafts, playing word games, and signing petitions to make a positive difference in the world, and...and so much more. I want to talk about how Desi's smile and their belief in me makes me feel like I can fly. Or how much I love my trans English teacher."

I gulp for air. "And how much I hate that a few vocal, organized people are mass banning books because they're racist and transphobic and queerphobic, unable to deal with mental health or survivors of abuse, and they don't want kids reading about real life or knowing they're not alone because hey, we might change the status quo, make it a better, more equitable world. And how they're trying to take away my rights with homophobic bills and laws." I take a deep breath, then another. It feels good to get that all out.

Mom keeps her gaze on me, nodding. "What else?"

"I want to tell you how scared I am when I'm really sick that

I'll never get to grow up or achieve my dreams. And how I don't understand some people wanting to kill others, or carry weapons that can kill and maim. Or make laws that hurt people who are different than them, or spew hate and bigotry. I'm one of those people who are different, Mom. I'm queer. Chronically ill. And I see visions of the future, and sometimes the past, whether you believe me or not." I pause to breathe.

"Wow," Mom says, reaching for my hand. "That's a lot. And—I think you're right. I have missed out on a lot by only focusing on your health. I just—I don't ever want to lose you." Her hand tightens on mine.

"I get it, Mom. But there's more than one way to lose someone—and never connecting with them on a deep level, never really talking about anything important beyond one thing, well, that's a huge disconnect."

Mom's lips tremble. "When did you get so wise?" She shakes her head. "I don't want to miss out on anything with you, honey. And I know my anxiety over your health can get in the way. So—let's make a plan to talk every weekend, okay? And whenever anything comes up."

I blink. I'd never put it together that Mom's obsession with my health, her constant checking on me, is because she has anxiety. I mean, I knew she worried about me, and I knew she didn't want me to die. But it's a new thought that my mom has anxiety. I wonder if it's inherited, because I'm not exactly a pool of calm.

"Okay," I say. "And you can talk to me about things, too, you know. Like your anxiety."

"You're growing up so fast," Mom whispers.

But I've always felt old. Well, ever since I almost died that first time.

"I promise I'll make an effort to not just focus on your health," Mom says. "But that means I need you to take your health seriously, to take your medications without prompting, to test your peak flow regularly, to sit things out when you need to, and to call when you have an attack."

"I will," I say. "I promise."

Mom squeezes my hand and lets go. "Good. Now tell me about Desi."

And for the first time in a long time I feel heard by my mom, and close to her. I can't believe how many good things are happening, things I never thought I'd have. Desi liking me back. Desi and their family believing me. Meeting another person with a paranormal gift. Mom actually listening to me about something other than my asthma. Mom giving me freedom, even if it's only an hour at a time.

And I think I can actually save Inez and Jenna—with Desi's help. Inez doesn't want to hurt her family, and I don't think she really wants to die; she just doesn't want to be in pain. And while Jenna won't listen to me, we're going to lure Mason away. Everything is finally going to be okay. No, better than okay. Things are going to be great.

I'm DOING MY HOMEWORK when my cell buzzes. I push my books aside on my desk, and pick up my cell.

Nana says you've got to start trusting your visions, Desi texts. **The spirits told her danger's coming.**

My chest tightens. **We know danger's coming,** I text. **We've already warned Jenna and Inez...**

That's what I said. But she still wanted me to tell you to trust your visions. It'll help you see more.

I chew my lip. **Ok. How's Inez?**

Holed up in her room. Trying not to worry.

I sit back, my chair squeaking. **I'm sorry. I wish I could help more.**

You already did, Desi texts. **How's Jenna?**

I sigh. **Still not opening up to me.**

That sucks. But don't give up. ...Nana's calling me. Later!

I set my cell down, and it clatters against my desk. I can't shake the sense that Nana was trying to warn me about something. Did I miss anything? I shiver, then cough.

But Jenna and Inez both know I think they're in danger.

My chest clenches and I cough again, my lungs spasming.

Damn. I grab my inhaler and take a puff.

"You okay, Kate?" Mom calls from downstairs.

"Fine! Just swallowed some water the wrong way!" I yell, then cough again. I jump up and close my bedroom door, then turn on my music while I cough again. I take another puff. No way am I going to worry my mom, not after what she told me about her mom dying. Not unless I actually need help.

I cough harder, my chest tight, my throat narrowing.

Mason sits slumped in a lawn chair outside a wood shack, a woman with short graying hair next to him. He aims his handgun at a glass beer bottle with a printout of my face taped to it, and shoots. The bottle explodes, fragments of amber glass scattering across the dirt and grass.

"I don't know what to do, Mom," Mason says. "She's getting between us."

His mother sucks hard on the cigarette dangling from her lips. "Well, I know what you're not gonna do. You're not gonna sit there and take it." She wags her wrinkled finger at him. "Nobody walks over my boy."

Mason straightens up. "You're right." He aims at another bottle and shoots, the bottle exploding.

"'Course I am," his mother says, patting his tanned arm. "You gotta fight back, take what's yours." She grabs his gun from him and shoots the rest of the bottles one by one, amber glass exploding into the air.

I gasp for air, coughing, and suck on my inhaler. Does Mason's mom know how abusive he is? Is she encouraging him to be violent with me, too?

I cough-shudder. But no mother would encourage that, would she?

I use my inhaler again, and my chest starts to loosen. I breathe in as deeply as I can without coughing, my music still loud. The vision showed me something about me. Does that mean I'm in danger?

My skin goose pimples. But it was a vision of Mason—and Mason's connected to Jenna. That's all it is.

I cough again, and use my inhaler.

Someone pounds on my door.

I jump, stuff my inhaler in my pocket, and turn down my music. "Yeah?" I call, my voice gravelly.

My door creaks open, and Mom pops her head in. "You all right?"

I clear my throat. "Sure. Why?"

She takes a step into my room. "You don't usually have your music on so loud," Mom says.

"Aw, leave her alone," Dad says from behind her. "She's a teen now. It's just like Jenna blasting her music to let off some steam."

For once I'm grateful for his dismissiveness.

A cough builds in my chest. I try to hold it back.

"You weren't upset by what I—by our conversation earlier, were you?" Mom asks.

I shake my head no, holding my breath and the cough in.

"Come on, Elizabeth, leave the girl alone," Dad says, tugging her arm.

I smile and waggle my fingers like Desi does.

Mom smiles uncertainly. "Well, if you're sure..."

Dad pulls her out of my room, and they close the door behind them.

I turn up my music and cough.

When I come down for breakfast Mom doesn't say anything about my breathing, my meds, or my peak flow meter, though her gaze keeps darting to my meter, and she takes deep breaths, her hands clenched around her coffee mug.

I decide to put her out of her misery, and grab my peak flow meter from the counter. "I already took my meds," I say.

I test my breathing—it's in the low green zone—and hold it out for her. "And my peak flow results are pretty good!" I sit down.

"They are," Mom says, her hands relaxing. "So, what's school like today? Do you see your—your trans teacher or your girl—joyfriend?"

She's trying. I sprinkle brown sugar on my oatmeal, and take a spoonful. "Yeah, both," I say. I look around the kitchen. "Dad already left?"

"Yes. I'll be glad when his presentation is over," Mom says, a tinge of sadness in her voice.

I wonder if she's lonely. "What's your day like?" I ask.

"Oh, I have two houses to show, and a client to check back in with, but I'm available any time if—" She stops herself abruptly.

"If I need you." I gulp my juice. "Thanks, Mom."

Mom smiles at me, a real smile.

I haven't needed her help with my asthma in a few days. It's been a relief not to have any bad attacks—but the attacks are my only way to know what's really going on with Jenna and Inez, whether we're on the right track or we need to do something different.

Maybe I should trigger another attack to find out. I spoon up more oatmeal. I can picture Desi and Nana looking at me disapprovingly. Or maybe I should try doing things Nana's way, especially if it means no asthma attacks.

I gulp down the rest of my oatmeal, then rinse out my bowl and put it into the dishwasher.

"What's the rush?" Mom asks.

"I forgot some homework I have to do."

"All right, but don't be too long or you'll be late," Mom says.

Upstairs in my room, I switch on my bedside lamp, then sit cross legged on my bed, breathing slowly, staring at a point on my wall. Nana said I have to meditate, and let go of my fear and doubt.

I try to let my mind drift, but worries keep creeping in. What if it's all just in my head, like Mom and Dad think? Or what if I'm right but as usual I can't stop it from happening?

I grit my teeth. No, my visions have all come true. And this time I have three people who believe me.

I tell myself that over and over like a mantra, but I keep seeing Jenna lying dead in Mason's arms, and Inez swallowing her pills. My heart pounds too fast and hard, quickening my breath.

I blink to clear my thoughts, slow my breathing again. I know my visions are real.... So why aren't I getting a vision now? I'm doing what Nana said. Well, trying to.

I shift position on my bed, trying to breathe slower and deeper, without controlling it or paying attention to it. Maybe it's my fear of not being able to help Jenna and Inez, like all the others.

I loosely focus on my wall. What did Nana and Desi say about the fear, besides that I have to let it go? That things will be different this time because I have help. Because they believe me.

I breathe in again, my heart slowing to a more normal pace. It's true; things are already different. I have three people who believe my visions, including Inez herself, and that's never happened before. That's got to mean I can change things.

I push out my breath. So how do I encourage a vision to come now that I've let go of doubt and fear? I frown. Nana said to let my thoughts go. "Later," I tell my thoughts. I focus back on my wall, breathing in, breathing out, following the rhythm of my breath.

"Wait!" Jenna cries, her arms raised in front of her. "It's not a bad thing—"
"The hell it isn't!" Mason yells.

The vision flickers out as quickly as it came. I reach for it, but it doesn't come back.

I punch my mattress. But I didn't have an asthma attack. I'm not even wheezing. Nana was right! I just need to practice more, and maybe I can get visions without having an attack.

"Kate!" Mom calls up the stairs. "Better hurry, or you'll be late."

18

MY WHOLE BODY FEELS lighter the instant I see Desi in the schoolyard, like gravity has let go of its hold on me.

They turn before I can call out and their eyes light up, their mouth creasing into a wide smile. We stride toward each other, and they lean in to kiss me, not caring who sees, their lips feathery soft. My breath shudders in my throat, and I pull them tighter to me, erasing the space between us.

I hardly notice the hoots, whispers, and laughter; I just keep kissing them, pulling them closer and closer, wanting to feel them against every inch of my body.

They pull me even closer, still, but break our kiss. "You feel so good, so soft," they whisper.

"So do you," I say, pulling in air.

"You sure you're not gonna elope?" Gabby yells.

Desi whirls on her, their fists clenched. "She is not her sister, just as you are not your mother, Gabby. Take some care before you spew your unhappiness onto others."

Gabby's mouth pinches, and she turns away.

I slide my hand over Desi's clenched fist. "Hey."

They open their hand, clasping mine, and take a deep breath before facing me. "I'm sorry. I hope I didn't embarrass you."

"No—I wanted to say thank you," I say. "You did that beautifully.

You always do."

"I did?" Desi says, their tight lips softening into a smile.

"Yep! Even when you're mad, you're kind."

Desi laughs. "I love that you see that in me."

"I think everyone does," I say. "Even when things are hard, you make me feel like they're not as bad as they could be."

The weight of the future comes back to me, settling on my chest, my heart.

Desi studies my face. "You worried we can't change things again?" they say.

I shrug. "I hope we can."

"Inez is still struggling, but she's talking to us. She wasn't doing that before you told me what you saw."

"I guess that's progress," I say. "Jenna's still not telling me the truth."

"But we'll have Mason out of the apartment at the time he was supposed to kill her," Desi says, hooking their fingers through my belt loops and pulling me closer. "Try not to worry. We've made a plan, and we can keep adding to it."

I want to snap that that's easy for them to say, but I know it's not. Their sister is in danger, too. And judging from the bags under their eyes, their sleep was as restless as mine. "We only have one day left," I say instead. "And all those other times—" I swallow hard, the faces of people I couldn't protect rushing through my mind.

Desi sucks in their lower lip. "I know," they say gently. "Hey—I was thinking about the blockages Nana mentioned. I think you also gotta forgive yourself for not being able to protect anyone—"

I slump my shoulders, my body heavy.

"Even though it wasn't your fault," they add. They frown, snapping their fingers. "There's something you said when you first warned me about Inez...a cop got the girl back that you saw?"

I straighten. "Yeah, she got Zoey back after she was abducted."

Desi's eyes widened. "That was you? You tipped off the cops?"

"Yeah." I shrug. "But I knew Zoey'd be kidnapped and no one believed me. She went through hell because of that."

"Kate—you saved her *life*," Desi says, gripping my arm. "You are freaking amazing. And you did it without support or anyone believing you. So forgive yourself for all the times no one heard you. You can't force people to believe you; you can only tell them the truth."

I close my eyes against the tears.

Desi kisses my eyelids, their mouth soft. "It's gonna be different this time; I swear. Now forgive your younger you, the girl who didn't have anyone believe her, or even any support." They pull me closer, wrapping their arms around me.

I lean my head against theirs. I see myself frantic by Nevaeh's hospital bed telling Nurse Sato they need to do something; warning Zoey at school that someone was going to try to snatch her and she needed to stay wary; telling our neighbor not to climb the ladder to his roof without someone to hold it. See so many more times.

I breathe in raggedly. "It wasn't your fault," I tell the little girl I was, the girl no one listened to. "You tried to protect them. You did the best you could. It wasn't your fault." I'm crying now.

Desi hugs me tighter, rocking me. "It wasn't your fault," they whisper, their voice blending with mine. "And you did save Zoey. You gotta take that in. She's alive because of you. You're a freaking superhero."

I snort and pull away, swiping at my eyes, the backs of my fingers bumping my glasses. "It wasn't my fault. And Zoey's alive...because of me."

Desi nods. "Damned right she is. You feel any better?"

"Some," I say.

"Some is better than none."

I laugh and swipe at my eyes again.

"It's all gonna work out," Desi says fervently.

I wonder if they're trying to convince themselves, too, and not just me. The stress of what could happen tomorrow is getting to us.

"Have you been practicing what Nana told you?" Desi asks.

"Yes," I say, my chest hot. At least I did today, even if it wasn't for very long. "I saw a flicker of a vision and didn't have any problems breathing."

"That's great!" Desi cries. "See? Things're getting better. You just gotta keep practising."

"Sure," I say, my voice clipped.

Desi pulls back to look at me. "What?"

"I only saw a flicker," I say. "And tomorrow is almost here. I don't think Nana's way is going to be enough."

Desi's lips tighten. "Are you suggesting you trigger an asthma attack?" They cross their arms abruptly. "Put your health at risk? No way!" They glare at me. "We've already talked to Inez, and we've set things up for you to be with Jenna. Why can't you just trust the process?"

"Because it never worked before!" I yell.

Desi throws up their hands. "Right! When you were alone. You keep forgetting you've got me and Nana and Inez. Or don't you believe in us, either?"

"It's not that," I say.

"Then what is it?"

"I just—I want to be prepared."

"We are. You are."

"But what if we've missed something? What if I have?"

"We haven't. You haven't."

"You don't know that," I say. "You only know what I noticed in my visions. What if I missed something important?"

"We have to trust what you see. That's what your visions are for. To guide you."

I want to scream. "But what if we don't have all the pieces? What if things have changed because of what we've done, and we don't know it? Are you willing to risk your sister's life?"

Desi glares at me, their lips trembling. "That's not a fair question. Of course I don't want Inez to die, or Jenna, either. But I also don't want you to, and you risk your life when you have an attack." They clench their fists. "Sure, I want another vision—but only if you can see it without setting off your asthma."

Desi jabs their finger at me, their eyes shimmering with tears. "Your gift doesn't mean anything if you're dead. You sure couldn't help anyone then." They take a deep, shuddering breath. "Let's just keep to the plan. We'll visit your sister tomorrow, then mine. And we'll keep them alive. Okay?" They reach out their hand, their brown eyes watching me steadily.

"Okay," I say reluctantly, and squeeze their hand. But if I need to, I will trigger a vision.

"Okay," Desi says softly, leaning in to hug me again.

My belly feels heavy, like I've swallowed a rock.

I keep worrying that I'm missing something. And Desi's right; I can't help either of our sisters if I'm dead. So I'll do it Desi and Nana's way. In science class I let my thoughts drift, focusing on my breathing, Mr. Noor's droning voice helping me drift further. I sink into my knowledge that my visions are true, and into the love and support Desi gives me.

Inez bows her head, dropping her phone onto her bed. "What does anything matter? Nothing will ever happen to them."

The vision fizzles out.

"Kate? Am I boring you?" Mr. Noor asks.

I blink. "Uh, no sir."

"Good. Then get your supplies from the front of the class and get to work."

I get up, my mind on the vision. Inez is still obsessed with her ex, her rapists, or both. I did miss something! And if I missed something with Inez, did I miss something with Jenna, too?

I collect my beakers and solution and walk back to my desk, replaying the fragment of a vision I saw and the others I've had, but I can't figure it out.

At lunch I lean in close to Desi. "I did miss something. We need to talk to your sister after school."

Desi's eyes go wide. "What'd you miss?"

"Part of Inez's despair is that she thinks her ex, or her rapists, will just get away with it. That there won't be any justice."

"I know she doesn't believe in our legal system, and she hates how prejudiced our society is, but—" Desi bites their lip. "That's not something to give up your life for. Then they've really won."

"Sure—but despair can eat at your happiness, at your wanting to stay. We should go talk to her again today."

"All right," Desi says heavily.

I wait for them to say that I was right, that I should trigger more visions.

Desi's head jerks up. "Wait—how do you know?"

"I spaced out in Mr. Noor's class and got a vision fragment."

Desi laughs. "I guess spacing out gets you into the same zone as meditating. Or it relaxed your mind enough for the vision to come. All we gotta do is sign you up for more classes that bore you. Or get you to watch a science documentary." Desi elbows my side. "Come on—what bores you the most?"

"Besides Mr. Noor's class? I don't know."

"Hey," Desi says, raising their voice to the others at the table. "What bores you? Enquiring minds want to know."

"Oh god, math," a gay boy says, flapping his hand in front of his face. "And straight boys talking about cars."

"Yes!" a queer girl says. "And recipes. And English class."

"Hey, I love cooking," another boy says. "And good food."

"English? That's my favorite," I say.

"Yeah, well we can't all have Ms. Hirano like you two lucky humans," she says, nodding at Desi and me. "What I wouldn't give to be in her class!"

They start chattering on, one boy about loving makeup and nail polish, another about cooking. I start to zone out again.

"Well, that wasn't much help," Desi says. "Sorry."

"No—I figured out something else that bores me. Talking about superficial things."

"Are you saying makeup, nail polish, and cooking are superficial?" Desi asks, their eyes twinkling. "Because for Alfonze it's breaking the binary, escaping toxic masculinity and hetero norms."

"Oh, I know," I say, swatting their arm, "But for me it's the opposite. Society pushes me towards those things, says it's all I should care about. Well, that and dating boys, marrying, having a family."

"Yeah, I get it," Desi says. "Though I like to wear the occasional loud makeup, 'cause fuck the system. I know who I am."

"I love how secure you are in your identity," I say.

Desi smiles, their eyes vulnerable. "I wasn't always that way. I had to work at it. It helped having a bunch of queer friends." They wave their hand around the table. "And a supportive family. You have that now, too, in us."

I do in Desi, and maybe I will with Inez, if she makes it through—no, when she makes it through. And the others at the table who've accepted me without question. "You think I have more to figure out?"

Desi shrugs. "I dunno. That's up to you. But if you do, we're here for you."

"Thanks," I say softly. "Did your nana accept you right away?"

Desi leans back and laughs. "Hell, no. Being lesbian and nonbinary took some explaining." They chug back their milk. "But my nana—she listens, she really listens, you know? And she asks questions when she doesn't understand. She even talked to Inez about it."

The laughter fades out of Desi's eyes, and they sit up straighter. "Inez did her best to explain. She's always tried to be there for me since our mamá left. I want to be there for her now."

"You will be," I say. "You are."

Desi pushes away their lunch. "I hope it's enough."

That's the first glimmer of doubt I've seen in Desi about our being able to change my visions. "You're not sure, either!" I say. "All that telling me everything will work out, but you don't really know."

Desi rubs their face. "I'm pretty sure. I believe what Nana said, that you wouldn't have these visions if you couldn't change them. But nobody can be sure of anything, not a hundred percent. And this is the first time we've worked together on this." They raise their head to look at me, their face bleak. "So I hope so. God, I hope so. It's such high stakes—my Inez, your Jenna. And I'll do everything I can to help you. But yeah—I don't know for sure."

I don't know what to say. I've never seen Desi look so dejected. They're always full of enthusiasm and hope, always the one encouraging me on. My lunch forms a hard lump in my stomach. "It'll be different this time, because you all believe me," I say, touching their knee. "If what I saw can change for anyone, it should for Inez. She knows we know and care."

Desi nods. "Yeah...."

"And she knows it'd devastate you and Nana. She heard my warning; she didn't just toss it aside."

"That's true." Desi sits up straighter. "And Jenna may not be talking to you about it, but she knows you know—and we're gonna get Mason outta there, so that should change things." Desi takes another gulp of milk, then wipes their mouth with the back of their hand. "Thanks, Kate. I feel better now."

But I feel worse.

I duck into the bathroom before class, lock myself into a stall, and pull out my cell. I know Jenna's got a shift at the bakery today, and Mason won't be there, though I know she's kept busy.

It hasn't worked to tell her I'm worried about her, or that I know Mason's abusing her. And her withdrawing isn't a good sign. I've got to try something else.

Jenna—could we talk? I text. **I could come by the bakery after school.**

I watch the little dots start and stop, start and stop so many times I want to scream.

I get why you're worried, Jenna texts, **But things are going to be different now.**

I stare at my screen. I can't believe she indirectly admitted Mason's abusing her. **Different how? Why?**

More disappearing and reappearing dots. I clench my teeth. This is more frustrating than texting with Mom.

I'll tell you Friday at dinner.

But Friday dinner could be too late.

Couldn't I just drop by the bakery? I'll buy something; I promise, I text. Because Jenna's boss doesn't like her taking breaks to talk to family or friends.

More disappearing dots. I picture her baking in the back kitchen, flour on her face and hands as she kneads dough or rolls out cookies, getting flour on her phone as she texts me, or maybe soap suds from loading the dishwasher.

Friday dinner, Jenna texts.

I push my breath out in a gusting sigh. I don't know how to help her, except for what Desi and I already set up. It'd better be enough.

19

I WALK WITH DESI toward their place, their hand in mine. Mom gave me an hour again—enough time to talk to Inez. I chew on my lip. If Inez dies, will my relationship with Desi last? It's gross to think that way, but I feel so good around Desi I don't want to lose them. If Inez kills herself Desi will blame me, or themself, or both of us. And we'll both feel so much guilt it'll tear us apart. I want to save Inez for herself; I need to—but I also don't want to imagine life without Desi, not when being with them makes me more glad to be alive than I've ever felt.

With Desi I don't feel like the sick kid, or the kid with visions everyone thinks are fake. They see and accept all of me. And I feel attractive, and wanted. They've helped me feel right about my visions on a deep level, like I'm finally using them the way I should, to help others.

I don't even care any more that I don't have a "normal" teenhood, or that I sometimes get bullied. Desi likes me and believes in me. And so does Ms. Hirano, and Nana and Inez—as long as we save her.

We have to. Because Inez is smart, sensitive, and queer. She's strong and loyal. And she loves her family fiercely, and they love her just as much.

"What're you thinking?" Desi asks, squeezing my hand.

"That Inez is great. ...And how much I like you."

Desi laughs. "I like you, too. Listen, I'm sorry I got all insecure before. I know we're going to change things. It's just that Friday's staring us in the face, and it hit me hard about Inez. We're closer than most families; we've had to be."

"You don't have to apologize," I say. "I'm insecure all the time."

Desi flashes me a grin. "I love how easily you admit stuff like that. It takes guts."

My heart lightens. Desi doesn't think I'm weak or needy! They think I'm brave. "You do, too. You just did."

Desi shakes their head. "Not like you do. You're emotionally honest."

"And you're not?" I say slowly, my body tightening.

"Oh, I am. But—I can fool myself with bravado and stubbornness and confidence into thinking things aren't as bad as they really are, or not admit how scared I feel until I'm staring it in the face. You, you stare it down all the time, and you admit it."

"Well, I feel like I can tell you most anything," I say. "And I hope you feel that way about me."

"Oh, I do," Desi says. "I told you how jealous I am of your gift—that's not something I could say to anyone else, not in a million years."

I raise my eyebrows. "Not even to your nana?"

"Especially not to her! It makes her sad thinking of my mamá running off, not able to deal with her gift. Of being the last one in our family with the gift." Desi hitches their shoulders.

"I'm sorry," I say softly, squeezing their hand. "I'll bet your nana would be able to hear you, though. She seems like a strong woman. I mean, if you wanted to talk to her about it."

Desi glances at me. "She is." They puff up their cheeks, then blow out their breath. "Mierda. Maybe you're right. Maybe..." They shiver. "Maybe I'll tell her. After we save Inez."

"Good."

When we get to their apartment, Inez is holed up in her room. We stand outside her closed door.

"You want to talk to her, or you want me to?" Desi whispers.

"Why don't we both?"

Desi knocks on Inez's door.

"Go away!" Inez calls.

"Kate's here," Desi says.

Inez heaves a loud sigh. Her bed creaks, then her footsteps shuffle to the door, and she opens it half way. She's back in black sweatpants and a baggy purple T-shirt, but her hair is combed, and at least the T-shirt is different, with "My bi-fi signal is strong" stamped across the front.

"You see something again?" Inez asks me. "Or is this a let's-talk visit?"

I shift my weight. "Both."

Inez opens the door wider. "Well, come in." She shuffles back to her bed and sits cross legged next to her pillow. Her room doesn't smell as badly as it did before, and her window blinds are halfway up, the windows open a crack. That seems hopeful. I sit in her desk chair again, and Desi sits on the floor. "I like your shirt," I say.

Inez looks down at her shirt, then smiles wanly. "Thanks. So...what'd you see?"

I rub my hands on my jeans. "It was just a fragment—but you were upset, thinking that nothing will ever happen to your ex, or maybe your..."

"Rapists," Inez says, raising her chin. "You can say it."

"Rapists," I say quietly. "So if you want justice or to speak out, we'll try to help."

Inez plunks her chin on her hand. "Abusers get away with their abuse so often, especially if they're white, cis, het men. Some women, too."

"Absolutely," Desi says. "It's wrong. So let's do something about it."

"How?" Inez asks, leaning back against the wall, her body sagging.

"We could post the truth about what they did to you," Desi says.

Inez shrugs. "Their word against mine. And mine is crap since they smeared me online."

"Then we could find something incriminating and post it—texts, chats, emails, whatever. Do you know your ex's password?"

Inez rubs her face. "I'm sure he's changed it."

"Maybe," Desi says, slapping their thigh. "But we could try."

"And he's friends with one of the rapists, right?" I say. "Maybe there'll be something on his phone."

"I don't know if I can face him," Inez asks. "Not even for that."

"You don't have to," I say. "There's still power in speaking out and being heard. If you say something on social media, people will notice. And have you thought about..." I hesitate. I hope I'm not pushing her or making things worse.

"What?" Inez says flatly. "Just say it."

"Maybe going to the police? I know most cops aren't good with sexual assault survivors, but maybe they'd charge your abusers."

Inez purses her lips. "Yeah—all those white male cops'll really listen to a Mexican girl like me. They'll side with the white dudes."

"You'd probably get a woman detective for something like this," I say.

Inez pulls her knees up to her chest, wrapping her arms around them. "I've thought about it; I keep thinking about it. But even if it gets as far as the courts—especially if it does—it'll be hell. Reliving my trauma in front of people who are judging me, some who won't even believe me, and the other side trying to make it look like it was my fault, or I wanted it—which most men and some women believe about rape victims."

Inez closes her eyes. "It makes me sick just thinking about it. The legal system isn't set up to help survivors; it's set up to protect white boys and men. To protect abusers and oppressors. Keep the system going."

Desi looks at me, their eyes wide and scared.

"You're right," I say, "It isn't set up for survivors, and it could be really traumatizing. We'll find another way."

"Yeah? Like what?"

I lick my dry lips. "Like—you tell your story to a reporter..." Inez pulls herself in tighter, "Even anonymously. Or—" I shift on the hard chair. "Or maybe it shouldn't be about them at all," I say slowly.

Desi quirks their eyebrows at me. "What do you mean?"

"Inez is the important one here, not those assholes. If it's too hard to confront them or talk about them, if it would just traumatize you more," I say to Inez, "Then what can we do to help you feel safer, happier? Could you take a self-defence course for women and nonbinary folks? I'd go with you if you want company. Maybe Desi would, too."

"You bet," Desi says, pumping their fist.

Inez nods her chin to her knees. "I guess. Maybe."

"Hey, you could learn some fancy new ways to kick them in las pelotas," Desi says.

Inez rolls her eyes, but her smile is a bit bigger this time.

"We could even teach Nana!" Desi says, laughter in their voice. "Can you imagine that?"

"Teach me what?" Nana says from the doorway.

Desi jumps. "¡Dios mio!" they cry. "You scared me!"

Nana clicks her tongue, her brown eyes twinkling. "Teach me what?" she says again.

"Yeah, Desi, teach her what?" Inez says innocently, raising her head, her smile wider.

"Uh—" Desi splutters, their cheeks darkening. "How to kick a guy where it hurts."

Nana looks at Inez, one hand on her hip. "You want to learn that? I will teach you."

Desi's splutters turn into laughter.

Nana turns on Desi. "What? You think men behave any better when I was young? I learned a few tricks. I show you both. Show all of you," she says, winking at me, too. "Okay?" She turns back to Inez, waiting.

Inez sits up straight, a real smile on her face. "Okay, Nana. Gracias."

"I should have thought to teach you," Nana says, her voice wavering.

Inez's smile slips.

No! Don't get all upset, not when Inez was starting to lighten up, I think at Nana, clenching my fists.

Nana's eyes snap to mine, then back to Inez's. "You will see—I am very good at paining las pelotas," Nana says, making a grab and twist motion with her hand. "Even if I am old, I never forget."

Desi bursts out laughing again, burying their face in their hands. "I can't, I just can't! I need to unsee that!"

Slowly, Inez starts to smile, and then she's laughing, too.

20

"She seemed better to me," Desi says as they walk me home. "Did she to you?"

"Yeah—but you should still keep an eye on her," I say.

"Of course," Desi says, sounding affronted.

They're so protective of the people they love. "I just want to make sure she's okay," I say. "That both our sisters are."

"I know," Desi says. "I think we made a difference today. We got her to laugh."

I kick a crumpled pop can down the sidewalk. "You did. I wish I'd helped more."

"I never would've thought to suggest she take self defence," Desi says, "Though now it's obvious. And while Nana and I keep checking in with her she didn't say anything to us about feeling despair that her abusers will get away with it."

"That's why you've got to keep an eye on her," I say. "She's still keeping things in."

Desi grabs my arm, pulling me to a stop. "I'm grateful every day for you, for the way you care so much about others, the way you try to help Inez so much even though she's not your sister."

Heat floods me. I pull away. A woman carrying groceries edges around us, and I step back to let her pass.

"What's wrong?" Desi asks, their eyebrows coming together, their soft brown eyes puzzled.

"I'm helping Inez because I care about her, and I want her safe," I say, pushing the words out through my tight throat. "But it's also because I don't want to lose you."

"How could you lose me?" Desi asks, frowning harder.

A bicyclist rushes past me on the sidewalk, so close his arm brushes me.

"If Inez died you might blame me," I say, the words like heavy rocks on my tongue. "And even if you didn't we'd both feel so guilty."

Desi lifts my chin to force me to look at them. "And you think that's bad?"

I nod, my face burning.

"I think it'd be bad if we didn't feel guilty if Inez died. I don't even want to think about the possibility, but it is part of being human. It means we care, and we want to help." They take a shuddering breath. "Your warning us gives us the chance to save Inez, to help her save herself, to grow closer to her, and to Nana, too, who has renewed purpose in helping Inez and in training you."

Desi touches my cheek. "And I don't believe that you wouldn't try to help Inez even if we weren't together. You told me before you even knew I liked you. You care, Kate—I feel it from you. It makes me like you even more."

"Yeah?" I whisper.

"Yeah." Desi kisses me softly, then pulls away to look at me. "Better now?"

"Better," I say, then kiss them again. I can't believe how lucky I am to have them care about me back, to see me and appreciate me. I smile into their kiss.

"When all this is over we need to do something together, something fun or relaxing, no stress involved," Desi says.

"Yeah!"

Desi grabs my hand and starts walking again. "What would your dream date be?" they ask.

"Probably not yours," I say.

"Now this I have to hear," Desi says, elbowing me in the side. "Come on, tell me!"

"Okay, you asked. A craft class we do together," I say.

"Okay," Desi says. "I can do that. It'd be fun. But that's it?"

"Then a yummy meal, definitely with dessert. Something chocolate."

"I can always do chocolate. That it?"

"Then a bookstore where we buy each other a book they choose." I hold up a finger before they can ask. "Then snuggling up on the couch together, reading. Lots of snuggling. Lots of reading."

"I love snuggling!" Desi says, a smile quirking at the edge of their mouth. "And reading. And would there be kissing?"

"Yes. And reminding each other why we like each other."

Desi sighs. "That sounds so good. We're going to have to have that date when all this is over."

"I'd love that," I say. "We could go to a used bookstore and make our own food, or get fast food."

"A girl after my own heart," Desi says, laying a hand on their chest. "Why would you think I wouldn't like that? I might not have come up with it, but it sounds great."

"What would your dream date be?" I ask, biting my lip.

"Oh, a game of laser tag, then going to a football match and eating hot dogs, then dancing at a gay bar with music so loud we can feel it in our bones."

A truck thunders past us, so noisy I have to wait to speak. Which is good, because I don't know what to say. I don't know if I could stand that—never mind keep up without having an asthma attack. I bite the inside of my mouth. They were willing to do my dream date; I should be willing to do theirs. But if we love such different things are we really compatible?

Desi bursts out laughing, and lets go of my hand. "The look on your face!" Desi laughs harder, their eyes streaming tears.

I scowl at them. A car honks loudly beside us, the driver yelling and gesturing at the car in front of him.

Desi gasps for breath. "I'm sorry; I was just joking. And I really needed to laugh, you know? It was either that or scream with the tension of everything that's going on."

I wrap my arms around myself, pulling inward. "Glad I could amuse you."

"Hey. No," Desi says, reaching for my arm. "It wasn't like that. Mierda. Inez says my sense of humor can be off sometimes. I just picked things I thought you'd dislike to tease you, but I thought you'd know I was teasing. I'm sorry. Forgive me?"

I take a deeper breath, relief filling me. "What would be your real dream date, then?"

Desi rubs my arm. "It doesn't matter what we do together, as long as I'm with you."

That sounds more like the Desi I know. Except... "But what would *you* enjoy? What would be fun for you? If you're not thinking about my asthma."

"We do have to think about it," Desi says. "But okay—dream date. Having a picnic with you in a park, talking about everything we care about, my head in your lap, or your head in mine. Maybe flying a kite or blowing bubbles or just lying together and reading, sharing our favorite quotes." They sigh. "Then playing a board game or D&D, just the two of us. Going to Drag Night bingo or a queer show, as long as there's no smoking. Then home to snuggle and kiss and go over the day."

I let my arms fall back to my sides. "That sounds nice, too," I say, relieved that it really does.

"Doesn't it?" Desi smiles dreamily at me. "I want to do all the things with you, Kate. Everything you want to do and everything you can do without setting off your asthma. And if there's things you don't want to do or can't, we'll find something else. Okay?"

This is the Desi I know. The kind, compassionate Desi.

Wind chimes tinkle music from a house we pass.

Desi reaches for my hand. "I shouldn't have teased you, not when you've had others bully you. I'm sorry. And I'd never want you to do anything that made you uncomfortable or that could trigger your asthma, okay? That'd make things miserable for both of us."

"Okay..." I bite my lip. "It's just—it didn't feel good when you teased me."

"I know. I'm sorry. I won't do it again," Desi says. "I try to laugh to keep from screaming or crying when things are hard—but never at someone else's expense, and never at yours. I swear. Inez and I used to tease each other all the time, but we knew it was teasing. I'd never hurt your feelings on purpose."

"Okay," I say, relief feeling me. "I get needing to laugh to release emotion. But you know you can scream or cry with me, right?"

"Yeah," Desi says, squeezing my hand, then letting go. "You make me feel safe." They shake their head. "Next time I'll just tell you, okay? Sometimes I go down to a subway station and scream when the train screeches in."

"Sometimes I scream into my pillow when things are hard," I admit. "No one can hear because it's muffled."

Desi laughs. "Look at us—getting out our emotions in healthy ways. My Nana would be so proud." Their face gets serious. "I wish Inez would do that more. She holds things in too much; it's not good for her."

"Yeah." I take a breath. "I wish Mason would learn how to get his anger out in a healthy way, instead of hurting Jenna. And that Jenna would open up to me and trust me to help. I'm scared, Desi. Jenna said things are going to get better for her. I think she believes that Mason will just magically change."

Desi shakes their head, their stride longer. "She's deluding herself. But we'll get Mason outta there tomorrow, and you'll have a talk with her. Maybe she'll listen to you this time."

"Maybe." But my dread is back.

21

MOM'S STANDING AT THE kitchen counter chopping up peppers when I walk in, a pot of boiling water and another of sauce simmering on the stovetop. She turns and looks at me, her glance darting to my spare puffer, my nebulizer, my peak flow meter, then back to me, and I know she's struggling not to say anything. "You have a good time with Desi?"

"Yeah," I say, setting my backpack on the floor and grabbing some orange juice from the fridge and a glass from the cabinet. "And their family makes me feel at home." I pour my juice and take a gulp, savoring the icy cold sweetness.

"Good," Mom says, turning back to the counter to chop the rest of the peppers. "They should. It's almost time for dinner, so I won't offer you a snack."

"Could we invite Jenna over tonight?" I ask, taking another gulp of juice and sitting at the table.

Mom stiffens, then chops faster. "It's too late to invite her; you know that. Why're you pushing this? I told you I'd talk to her. That your dad will."

I set my glass down, my fingers cold. Do I tell her—even if she probably won't believe me? I clear my throat. "Mason's going to kill her tomorrow," I say to her stiff back.

Mom whirls around, her knife pointed at me, a piece of red pepper falling to the floor. "Don't even joke about that."

"I'm not! I told you; Mason beats her, and he's going to kill her tomorrow afternoon. We have to help her escape."

Mom drops her knife on the counter. "You think I haven't tried?" she asks, bowing her head.

I gape at her. "You—"

Mom wipes her hands on a dishrag. "Mason's fanned her resentment against your dad and me, stirred up her insecurities and kept her from seeing us often. But Jenna will hear no wrong about him, and my efforts have only pushed her farther away."

I blink. "So—you believe he's abusing her?"

"I didn't say that. But he is encouraging her to distance herself from us and that's not healthy, no matter what your dad says. We need family, people who care about us. Isolation isn't good for anyone."

I stare at her. She's never opened up to me like this before. My asking her to see me as more than my asthma seems to have changed things between us.

Mom sighs and leans back against the counter. "Your dad even accused me of interfering with Jenna, of being jealous. I ask you! Does that sound like me?"

I don't know. But I can't say that. "Couldn't you just say you really need to talk to her tonight?" I ask. "Even after dinner? I know you don't believe me, but it's true; Jenna's in danger."

"Kate," Mom says, sitting down at the table with me and touching my hand. "Don't work yourself up. You know that can set you off. You've been doing so good this week."

I rip away. "You're not hearing me! Jenna's going to die tomorrow!"

Mom puts her head in her hands. "Oh, Katie..."

The front door slams and Dad strides into the kitchen, setting down his briefcase. "What's all this?" He looks back and forth between us.

"Nothing," Mom says, jerking her head up. "We were just—"

"You have to get Jenna to come over tonight, Dad," I say. "Or it'll be too late."

Dad lowers his bushy eyebrows. "Too late for—"

"Mason's going to kill her," I say.

"That's enough!" Dad shouts, his neck and ears reddening. "I've had it with your attention-seeking lies. Go to your room until you can apologize to me and your mother." He clenches his fists. "You won't have supper tonight; maybe an empty stomach will make you think about your behaviour, if nothing else will."

I freeze, my breath fluttering in my chest.

"Ian," Mom says, her voice tight. "Don't be so hard on her."

Dad snorts. "We're not being hard enough on her. She has to learn she can't get away with lying. She's gone too far this time."

Dad steps closer to me. "I know you haven't had it easy being sick so often," he says, gentling his voice, "But this is not the way to get attention. Now go to your room. I expect an apology and a commitment to better, more mature behavior in the future before you come out."

I glance at Mom. She looks away, her eyes still watery. She doesn't believe me, either.

I knew it was a slim chance but she said she'd listen to me, and I had to try. I scrape back my chair and stand, then march up to my room. No way do I want to apologize for telling the truth. But I need to get out of here tomorrow to help Jenna and Inez. I wait an hour, until I'm sure Dad's had his dinner and a chance to cool down, until I hear him cheering for his team on TV. I wait for a commercial, then go down and meekly apologize for saying what I did.

Dad begrudgingly accepts my apology, then turns back to the game. He doesn't seem to notice that I didn't apologize for lying—because I didn't. I turn to go, but Mom points to the kitchen. She's put the leftovers in a bowl in the fridge. I eat it cold. I text Jenna again, but she doesn't answer.

22

I WAKE UP FRIDAY morning with dread weighing down my chest and prickling over my skin. It takes me a moment to remember why. Today's the day Jenna and Inez are supposed to die.

When I get to the schoolyard Desi's there, laughing loudly with their friends. They see me and come over, their body tight, their movements jerky. They grab me in a tight, almost desperate hug, and I hold them back, rocking them gently before letting go.

"Nana tried to stay with Inez, but Inez said she didn't need a sitter," Desi says, blowing out their breath in a shudder. "So she's camped outside Inez's door."

"Inez knows you both care, and that you need her. It's going to be okay," I say, hoping that's true.

Desi nods tightly. "Jenna?"

"She wouldn't agree to come over early, just said to wait until dinner tonight, and I'd see."

"We got this," Desi says, pulling me to them again.

I wrap my arms around them, leaning into their warmth. I'm not sure if I'm the one trembling or they are. Maybe it's both of us. "We got this," I whisper back. Because we have to.

All through my classes, I can't stop worrying about Jenna—whether I'll be able to stop Mason from killing her, or whether he'll just try again some other day. I don't know how to do this right—if there even is a right way. I'm just grateful Desi will be with me. Maybe together, we'll be able to save both our sisters.

I shift on the hard chair, trying to tune into Mr. Santos's mumbly voice as he drones on about algebra. He paces in front of the whiteboard as he talks, stabbing at the figures with his marker, but I can hear the boy behind me snoring quietly. I slide my mini word-search book out of my backpack, open it inside my textbook and search for words, circling each one I find. If Jenna knew what was going to happen today, she'd leave Mason. But there's no way I can convince her, not without letting it happen.

How do I keep it from happening again and again? If I stop Mason today, will that be the end of it, because he never meant to kill her? And how will I know if she's in danger again without having another vision? How do I even know if she'll be safe today? I circle words faster. If I trigger another attack, I might see something that'll help. But Desi's right; I can't help her if I'm dead.

Inez needs people to care about her, to help her stay safe, too. And so do all the people I'll have visions about in the future.

A shadow falls over my desk. I look up to see Mr. Santos watching me, his black hair slicked back, his glasses sliding down his nose. "Did you understand the lesson?"

I sit up straighter. "Yes, sir."

"Are you feeling ill?"

"No, sir."

Mr. Santos plucks the word-search book from my hands. "Then

get to work, please."

I bend over my notebook and start writing down numbers. Mr. Santos watches for a moment before he moves on. I focus on my work, but I can't stop worrying.

I bite the end of my pencil. Maybe I *should* try to trigger an asthma attack to make sure Jenna's okay. If the universe knows Desi and I are planning to stop Mason today, will it show me anything different?

Mr. Santos coughs, looking pointedly at me.

I scribble nonsense numbers in my binder, trying to look like I'm still working. I don't know how any of this works, but I can only push my body so far. And I'm taking a risk every time I trigger my asthma. I don't want to die, or get sent home or to hospital because I triggered a vision, and then not be able to help Jenna and Inez. I'd better wait to see what happens when I go see Jenna. Surely it'll be enough.

And maybe Dad and Mom can talk some sense into Jenna if she tells them the truth about Mason abusing her. Maybe they can get her to come home, or go to a shelter if she wants her independence so badly. If she wants to stay away from me.

I scribble over the nonsense numbers in my binder, ripping a hole through the page. I wish Jenna didn't resent me so much. Wish we could do things together—watch a movie in a theatre, go camping, eat ice cream together while we laugh or cry, the way I imagine sisters do. Instead she acted like a mini-mom, only concerned about my asthma, or shut me out completely, slamming her bedroom door in my face, turning up her music so she couldn't hear me cough, then raging when Mom or Dad made her turn it down so they could hear me if they needed to. The number of times she looked at me with rage in her eyes, or complained about my asthma affecting her life, are like a cold, sharp needle in my side.

I love Jenna—she's my sister—but I'm not sure I like her. And I'm definitely not sure that she likes me.

I wonder if we'll ever be close. I long for it.

I keep checking my cell as the day stretches on, the sound on vibrate. Two o'clock, five after two. The seconds tick by agonizingly slowly. I can't stop worrying that I'm timing it wrong.

At two-ten Desi texts me. **We're got a problem.**

I stare at my cell, my heart pounding too hard. Are they not coming with me? Did something happen to Inez? Or—

Mason pulled out of the car repair.

Shit! Why? Did you email him back?

Yeah. I told him it was the only time I could come by when I'm in the area, but...

I bite my lip, watching the screen. **But what?**

He said something more important came up.

More important than working on his dream car?

I know. I couldn't believe it either.

You think he's onto us? I text.

Maybe? But he did write to tell us he couldn't make it.

Shit. We need to get over there now.

On it. I'll meet you outside.

I start coughing and force a wheeze.

Mrs. Levi, always alert, comes to my desk. She touches my shoulder reassuringly. "Do you need to go to the nurse?" she asks.

I nod, feeling guilty about lying to her. I hope she doesn't remember that today's the nurse's day off.

"All right," she says, looking around the room.

"I can take her!" Zoey says, grabbing her bag and standing.

"I can go myself," I say. But Mrs. Levi insists.

Zoey and I walk through the halls together. I cough a few times to keep up appearances, but not very hard. I don't want to trigger a real attack. Zoey looks at me anxiously, and my chest burns hot.

"Hey," Zoey says, touching my arm, "Any time you need help, ask me, all right? I owe you big time."

"You don't owe me anything," I say awkwardly.

"No, I do. I never even thanked you properly."

"It's okay. You don't need to."

Zoey shakes her head hard, her locs hitting my cheek. "Yeah, I do. If you hadn't sent those tips to the cops I might never've been found. I might be dead. Or still being..." She shudders. "I was all traumatized after I got back. Still am. But damn, I've meant to tell you for ages I'm grateful. You gave me my life back. Thank you for helping me. For not giving up."

My eyes burn. She's right; I couldn't stop her abduction, but I did help bring her home. My visions did. "I'm glad you're safe."

"I wish I'd listened to you that day you warned me."

"I would've been surprised if you did." I shrug. "I know I sounded crazy. Most people don't believe my visions when I tell them."

"I do now," Zoey says, her voice deep with emotion. "Seriously. Thanks."

"You're welcome." I stop at the nurse's office. "We're here."

"But the nurse isn't in! Lemme take you to the office."

Shit. "It's just down the hall. Really, I'm okay."

"It's no bother," Zoey says and smiles.

I know she's just being nice, but I want to scream. I should be leaving *right now*.

Zoey walks me into the office. Mrs. Wang looks at me and picks up the phone. "Another attack?"

"Don't call my mom; I'm getting better!" I plead.

Mrs. Wang shakes her head. "No can do. You know the rules."

Right. Rules that my mom enforced. How am I going to get out of this one?

"I hope you feel better fast," Zoey says, and leaves.

I sit in one of the waiting chairs, my mind racing. I *have* to get to Jenna. Maybe I should duck out to the bathroom. I cough half-heartedly.

The principal calls Mrs. Wang into her office. I wait until the door closes then rush out into the hall, my heart pounding so hard I really am having trouble breathing. I push through the heavy doors and down the steps. A hand grips my arm.

23

"What took you so long?" Desi asks.

"Asthma story didn't work so well." I check my cell. Two-thirty. Only fifteen minutes before it'll be too late! "Come on!" I gasp, and start running. I speed dial Jenna but she doesn't pick up.

Desi runs beside me. "Is it far?"

"Maybe ten minutes walk from here." My breath rasps in my throat. I cut across the road, dashing between cars who honk at me, and onto the other side.

Desi grabs my hand, yanking me back. "Cab!" they yell, waving their other hand, and the cab screeches to a halt in front of us. We scramble in and I give Jenna's address.

"Please hurry!" I say. I lean forward, clutching the back of the front passenger seat, swearing silently at all the traffic. But I know we're faster in the cab than on foot.

The cab driver pulls up outside Jenna's apartment building.

"Go!" Desi says, opening their wallet. "I'll meet you inside."

Only five minutes left. "Her apartment is six-oh-five!" I stumble out of the cab, run into the building, and slap the elevator button. "Come on, come on!" I say. The doors open.

I rush in and ride up to the sixth floor, my tongue sticking to the roof of my mouth. I race down the hall to Jenna's apartment. Mason yells, his voice muffled behind walls, and then there's a thud.

I pound on the apartment door. "Jenna!" I shout. "Jenna, it's Kate!"

A little dog yips in one of the apartments. Down the hall, an old woman opens her door and pokes her head out to stare at me, her grey hair in curlers.

It's too quiet in Jenna's apartment. *Don't let me be too late!* I pound on the door again. "Jenna!"

There's silence, then footsteps click against hardwood. Jenna opens the door, her face pale. "Katie? What're you doing here?"

Relief fills me. "Jenna." I wrap my arms around her tight. Her heart pounds hard against my chest, like she's been running. Or maybe it's my heart.

"Katie?" Jenna says again. "Shouldn't you be in school?"

I don't know what to say to that. I only thought about getting here in time.

The floor creaks and Mason appears behind Jenna, his shirt half open, his face flushed. "Kate—you really need to call first," he says, smiling awkwardly.

Oh god. Did I catch them doing it? But that can't be right. Unless my visions are wrong. But no, I heard him yelling, heard a thud.

I stare at Jenna. Her neck is reddened right where I "saw" Mason jam her against the wall, and her body looks tight like she's ready to run.

"What do you want, Kate?" Mason asks impatiently.

Desi runs down the hall and skids to a stop next to me, panting.

"Who's this?" Mason asks. "Did Jenna know you were both coming?" He puts a hand on her back.

I don't want to make it worse. "No, I—" I can't think fast enough. I scramble in my bag and pull out another mini word search book. "I brought a peace offering," I say, handing it to Jenna.

Jenna takes it, blinking rapidly. "Thanks?"

Why, oh why didn't I plan this out more? "You two still coming over for dinner?" I ask.

"Yes," Jenna says.

"*That's* why you dropped by? To make sure we were coming to dinner?" Mason asks, his eyes narrowing. "You could've just texted."

I grab Desi's arm. "Well, I wanted you to meet someone," I say to Jenna, "My joyfriend. Desi."

"Joyfriend?" Desi says.

"Uh—datefriend? Datemate?" I say.

They laugh. "I like datefriend the best. Though joyfriend is nice, too. We should've figured out what to call it before this," they say, a smile curling their lips.

Jenna's eyes brighten. "You're dating? You didn't tell me! Good to meet you, Desi. I'm Jenna, Kate's sister." She puts out her hand.

"Good to meet you, too," Desi says politely, shaking her hand. "Kate's told me all about you."

"Yeah?" Mason says, narrowing his eyes at me.

"Yeah," I say quickly. "We traded stories about our sisters."

"Who's your sister?" Jenna asks a little too brightly. "Would I know her?"

"I think so," Desi says. "Inez Flores. She's about your age."

"Inez.... We used to hang sometimes," Jenna says, her voice trailing off.

Used to. She doesn't do most of the things she used to do, especially if they involved other people or going places.

"Maybe we could all go out sometime!" I say.

Jenna raises her eyebrows at me. "And do what?"

"We could, I don't know, go roller skating or go to a concert."

"I don't do that kind of thing any more," Jenna says. "And you never do."

"Well, we could, babe," Mason says.

"Yeah?" Jenna says, standing taller, her smile more real.

"Yeah. You and me. Make it a date night," Mason says, kissing her cheek. "You deserve to have some fun."

Ugh. If I didn't know better from my visions I'd think he's a good guy, or at least not abusive.

A door opens down the hall, and the same old woman with curlers in her hair pokes her head back out to frown at us, then snaps her door shut. I shift my feet. It's awkward standing out in the hall, not being invited in, but it doesn't matter, not as long as it keeps Jenna safe. Have we managed to stop Mason from killing her?

I discretely check my cell. It's two forty-five—exactly when Jenna died. But she's right here, looking at me strangely. I wish I knew more how this works, if getting her past the time of her death is enough, or if we need to do more.

"Did you tell Mom and Dad yet?" Jenna asks me. "About your new girl—I mean datefriend?"

"I told Mom," I say, stuffing my hands into my jeans. "Maybe she told Dad? I don't know. We haven't had the big meet-the-parents thing yet. I, uh, wanted to tell you first. I wasn't sure how Dad'd react," I say glibly.

Jenna frowns at me. "You already came out to them. It was another big Kate moment, overshadowing my hockey win."

God, everything's a competition to her for our parents' attention. I swallow tightly. "I didn't mean to take away from your big triumph," I say. "Mom found the rainbow flag in my room, and I couldn't hide it any longer."

"Wait—your parents aren't okay with you being queer?" Desi asks. "I thought you said they were."

"No, they are," I say. "They just needed time to get used to it. My dad especially. But I'm not sure how he'll react to my actually dating someone. Jenna's the only one who dated, and—" I bite my lip.

"And I eloped," Jenna says, still too brightly.

"Best day of our lives, right babe?" Mason says, squeezing her shoulder.

"Absolutely," Jenna says.

"And they don't like me doing much of anything on my own because of my asthma," I tell Desi. I turn to Jenna. "So, um, how do you think Dad'll take it?" I ask.

"I don't know," Jenna says slowly.

"Maybe you could smooth things over for me?" I say. "Dad listens to you."

"I guess I could," Jenna says, like it's a huge favor to ask.

It's past the time Mason killed her—and she's still here. Did we keep them distracted long enough? "I sure would appreciate it," I say.

"And that," Mason says, pointing his finger at me, "Has got to be the real reason you're here, right? To ask Jenna to work things out with your dad for you. Even though she's got her own issues with them. Right Kate?"

"Mason," Jenna says, resting her hand on his hairy arm.

"Issues?" I say, looking back and forth between them. "What is he talking about?"

"Oh, come on," Mason says. "You can't be that obtuse. Your parents fawn all over you if you so much as cough, but Jenna twists her ankle at a game and they tell her to shake it off."

"They do?" I say, staring at her.

Jenna shrugs. "Dad did. He's never been that good with emotions or my getting hurt."

"Or me getting sick," I say.

"Yeah," Jenna says softly.

And Dad's the one she's closest to. So how would he react if she told him Mason was hurting her?

I push my breath out. "You don't have to talk to him for me, Jenna. I'm just glad you're coming over to dinner. I miss you. We all do."

"Thanks," Jenna says, her voice wobbly. She leans over to hug me fast before letting me go, almost pushing me away, wincing.

"You, uh, you want to do something, the four of us, before dinner tonight?" I ask.

"Can't," Mason says. "We got stuff to do. Right, babe?"

"Right," Jenna says brightly.

"Okay." I shift from foot to foot. "Well, I meant it—I'm looking forward to seeing you. And you really don't have to talk to Dad for me. Just having you home again is good."

"I'm right here, you know," Mason says, scowling.

God, I hope I haven't made things worse. "We all want you there, too," I say quickly. "I know how much Jenna loves you; you're all she talks about. You're part of our family." As much as I wish he wasn't.

Mason nods, his face relaxing. "Damn right I am."

"Kate's told me about you both, how important you are to her," Desi says, ducking their head briefly like they're shy. "So it meant a lot to me that she'd introduce me to you."

Nice save. I smile at them.

Jenna raises her eyebrow. "You could've just brought them to dinner."

"And have our parents swarm all over them? We're not ready for that yet," I say. "You're the ones I wanted them to meet."

"I hope you keep this one out of trouble," Mason says, jerking his chin towards me. "She always takes on more than she can handle. Wouldn't want her to get hurt."

I swallow tightly. Was that a threat?

"Kate can be real naïve," Mason continues, scratching his cheek, the rasping sound loud. "So maybe you can help her with that, too. Like I know when I'm being scammed; I got this offer to work on my dream car today." His cold gaze stabs mine, steely anger vibrating off him, then flits back to Desi.

Desi stiffens. I struggle to breathe normally.

"But I saw right through it. Not sure Kate here could, though." Mason puts his arm around Jenna and pulls her close, smiling at us with his teeth bared. "And nothing'd take me away from time with my girl."

My hands feel cold, as if I've been dunked in a frozen lake.

"It was nice to meet you, Desi," Mason says. "But next time," he says, looking at me, "Call before you drop by."

"Oh, um, sorry," I say.

"See you tonight," Mason says firmly.

"Yes, see you later!" Jenna says brightly as Mason steps back, pulling her with them, and closes the door.

Desi looks at me, their eyes wide, and tugs me back down the hall.

"Did we do enough?" I ask quietly.

"I hope so," Desi whispers. "I got really bad vibes from him. And shit—he knew! He knew it was us."

"I know," I whisper. "How the hell did he know?"

"I don't know," Desi says. "Maybe we laid it on a little too thick about his favorite car."

I shiver. Did we just make things worse?

24

"Thank you for coming with me," I tell Desi as we walk down the street. "And for backing me up."

"Of course," Desi says. "And we made it on time."

"Yeah, this time. But how do I know if I stopped him from killing her for good? How do I keep it from happening again? What if I don't get a vision the next time she needs help?"

Desi looks at me sharply. "What're you saying?"

"I don't know—except that she has to get out of there."

"Yeah," Desi says. "If she doesn't, it'll probably happen again."

That's what I'm afraid of.

"But you can't force victims to leave," Desi says. "They have to take it at their own pace. Just keep supporting her. She'll get there."

I hope so. And what about Inez? Will talking to her, letting her know we care, be enough? I pull out my cell. Nine messages, all from Mom.

Crap. I call her. "Mom, I'm okay," I say fast.

"Where've you been?" Mom says, her voice sharp and high pitched. "I've been frantic!"

"I'm so sorry. I was worried about Jenna; I had to make sure she was okay."

"But the office said—"

"It was a misunderstanding. I'm okay. I'm not even wheezing. I'm so sorry, Mom. Really. I just got distracted by Jenna. I never meant to worry you."

Mom's silent for a moment, and I know she's listening to make sure.

"Desi can tell you I'm okay. Here." I hand the phone to Desi.

"Mrs. Robbins?" Desi says, then listens. "Yeah, no, she's okay. She really was worried about Jenna; she was having a panic attack, so I thought if she saw Jenna it'd calm her down. I know that's better for her asthma. But we should've thought to text you," Desi says.

Smooth. And so close to the truth.

Desi listens, biting their lip. "Yeah, I know. I'm really sorry; we didn't mean to scare you. I promise she's okay. Yeah, sure." Desi hands me back the phone. "She wants to talk to you."

"Mom?" I say.

"Don't you ever do that to me again, Kate Robbins! Not ever. I was getting ready to call the police and ambulance, only I didn't know where you were or if you were okay." Her voice breaks.

"I won't; I promise I won't," I say. I can't risk her grounding me now, not when we still have to make sure Inez will be okay. Desi's frowning hard, biting their lip; I know they're worried, too. "I promise to always tell you if I'm in trouble, and you can even put a tracker app on my phone so you can keep tabs on me, okay?" I say. "I've just got to do one more thing—I need to go talk to Desi's sister; she's having a really hard time right now. And then I'll be home; I promise," I say.

Mom sighs loudly. "You have a good heart, Kate, and I'm glad for that—but you have to call me about something like this. You have to be more responsible."

"I will—I promise I will," I say. "But Inez needs me right now." I glance at Desi, raising my eyebrows, and they nod. "She was...she was raped, Mom, and she's not dealing with it well. I'll talk with her an hour, tops, and then I'll be home. Okay?"

There's a silence. "Fine. Be home in time for dinner," Mom says quietly, then hangs up.

I stare at my cell. I can't believe I got off that easy.

"Your mamá's overprotective?" Desi asks sympathetically.

"Yeah." I stuff my cell into my pocket. "I can't believe she let me go with you to see Inez after that."

"Maybe she was just relieved that you're all right."

"Yeah. Or maybe she's actually listening to me now, the way I asked her to." I nudge them. "Thanks for letting me tell her about Inez. I think it helped."

Desi shrugs. "She needs you there. And it's not like the whole school doesn't know."

We walk in silence for a few steps. "You and your sister don't get along that well?" Desi asks.

Of course they picked up on that. I shrug. "I've always been really sick, which means my parents spent a lot more time with me. My mom especially. Jenna...resents it."

"That sucks," Desi says.

When we get to their place, Nana is still sitting outside Inez's room in a kitchen chair. Inez doesn't want to let us in, telling us she doesn't need to be watched over, but when I tell her that I need her help with my sister, she cracks open her door.

"Jenna's in trouble?" Inez asks.

"Big time," I say.

Inez crinkles her nose. "Is it because of her boyfriend? I mean husband? He seemed like a control freak."

"Yep," I say.

"No surprise," Inez says. "Well, come on in and tell me what's going on." She opens her door wider. She's back in her black sweatpants and baggy T-shirt.

Nana stands stiffly and grips my arm. "You are a blessing," she whispers. "I am going to make tea," she says louder, and walks off.

I enter Inez's room, Desi close behind me. The blinds are pulled down again, the windows shut, the air stuffy. Inez's hair is messy, her shirt stained, her body held stiff like she's afraid she might break.

"But I don't need a minder," Inez says. "I'm doing okay."

"Yeah, we can see that," Desi says.

Inez raises her middle finger at Desi, then plops down onto her bed, Desi beside her. I sit in her desk chair again. Inez jerks her chin at me. "So, what's Jenna's jerk of a husband doing?"

"He's beating her, but she won't admit it," I say.

"Wow. That's awful."

"Yep. But no matter what I say, she won't admit what's happening."

Inez rubs her tangled hair. "Sometimes people can't deal with reality, you know? So they deny it, try to shut it all out..."

I wonder if she's talking about herself. "Yeah," I say. "Jenna's been denying reality a lot. Making excuses for Mason."

"Our papi, he used to beat our mamá, too," Inez says. "And she did the same thing, excused his behavior, said it wasn't so bad, even when she was standing there with a black eye and a tooth knocked out."

Desi stares at her. "He did? She did? Dios mío, I didn't know!"

"Yeah, you were too little to remember." Inez closes her eyes, shuddering, then opens them again to stare bleakly at me. "It was bad. He didn't like her gift. But when he died she grieved so hard. I never understood why." She rubs her arms. "She withdrew into herself after that, shut out Desi and Nana and me."

"Kind of like you've been doing," I say softly.

Inez scowls at me, jutting her chin out. Desi rests their hand on her back, and Inez softens. "Yeah," she says quietly. "Kind of like I've been doing." She turns to Desi. "I'm sorry, Carnala. I never meant to do that."

"Hey, it's okay," Desi says, hugging her. "Just...don't keep shutting us out, okay? We need you."

Inez leans into Desi, resting her head on their shoulder and sighing. "Yeah. I need you, too."

Desi strokes Inez's tangled hair. "Good. 'Cause we need you around for a long time."

Inez nods into Desi's shoulder. She looks softer than when we first came over, less brittle. Like she's actually taking in some of the comfort Desi's offering. I wish Jenna would do that. Wish she'd let me in.

Inez kisses Desi's cheek, then pulls back to look at me. "There's something else, isn't there?"

I rub my hands on my jeans. Do I tell her, or don't I? But she's already thinking about killing herself. We've talked about death. I don't see how this can make it worse. "I saw her husband kill her," I say. Inez jumps. "In my visions."

Inez blows out her breath. "Wow. That's heavy. And she won't listen to you?"

"Nope. My family doesn't believe in my visions, not like yours does."

"So how can I help?" Inez asks.

"I don't know..." I really don't. "She was supposed to die today..." Inez jumps again. I grip my hands together. "Maybe you could text her? Check in with her?"

"Out of the blue?" Inez says, raising her eyebrows. "Jenna and I weren't exactly chummy. We sat in some of the same classes, had the occasional group hangout at the roller-skating rink, a pizza joint, a concert."

I hadn't really meant to ask Inez for help, but now that we're talking I think it could be good for them both. Get Inez out of her own head and focused on helping someone else, and connect Jenna to some old classmates, remind her of the things she used to do.

I lean forward. "But if you could remind her of that, invite her to do something again, maybe she'd remember how things used to be before Mason took over her life. She's so isolated right now."

Inez pushes her hair out of her face. "Okay. I'll text her. No promises she'll text back, but...I'll ask to catch up. Say that I've been thinking about her, especially since you and Desi are dating."

"Perfect!" I say. "And you'll do it before tonight? She's coming over for dinner, and she's deep in denial."

"I'll do it when you leave," Inez says.

I get up and hug her, and she squeezes me tight. "You'll make a difference for Jenna; I know you will," I say. "And helping someone like that, that's huge."

Inez pulls back. "Laying it on a bit too thick there."

"But it's true," I say.

"Yeah, yeah," Inez says.

"Helping someone, letting them know you care, can make all the difference," Desi says, their voice choked up. "Thinking you're alone in your fight can be too hard for anyone."

Inez rolls her eyes.

"Inez—I need you around," Desi says, their voice hoarse.

Inez grips Desi's shoulder. "I know you do. I need you, too. We've gotten through everything together."

"Yeah, we have," Desi says.

Inez smiles at them tremulously, then jerks her chin at me. "I'll try to reach Jenna; I promise. It's too hard to go through painful things alone. I'm really lucky to have this one for a sibling." She pushes Desi's shoulder. "And our nana for family."

"Thank you," I say. I study her. She still looks washed out, but there's a little more spark in her attitude. "And you'll reach out to me or Desi or your Nana if you need someone?"

"Aw, get out of here," Inez says, shoving me, but she smiles wanly. "Yeah, I promise."

25

DESI WALKS ME BACK to my street, stopping at the corner to kiss me gently. "Thanks for giving Inez a focus. She needed that."

"It might help them both," I say.

"Yeah." Desi's face clouds over. "I can't believe she never told me about mamá getting beaten. That must've been a lot for her to carry."

I touch their cheek. "And you? How're you doing with it?"

Desi shrugs. "It's a weight. It's heavy, you know? But you got Inez to open up about it. That's hopeful. I think we've passed the crisis point for them both. I hope we have, anyway."

"Me, too," I say fervently.

Desi kisses me again, pulling me to them, their kiss filled with the same urgency and fear I feel. I kiss them harder, grip them tighter, my body trembling.

Desi pulls away. "Hey, it's gonna be okay," they say, cupping my cheeks with their hands.

"Sure," I say, a warm tear trailing down my cheek.

"We changed things today," Desi says. "I'm sure of it." They kiss my cheek, my forehead. "Now get home before your mamá freaks out."

I snort. "Too late for that. Though you did calm her down." I kiss them once more then start up my street, my feet dragging. Mom's car is parked in the driveway. I am so not looking forward to the lecture, though I know I deserve it.

A cool breeze chills the warmth from my skin, the sky turning a gun-metal gray.

A black pickup-truck door swings open so close it brushes my side.

I jump back as Mason gets out, blocking my way. I curse myself for not noticing.

"Sorry, Kate. Didn't mean to scare you," Mason says, holding up his grease-stained hands. "Can we talk a minute?"

I look over my shoulder but Desi is already gone, the street deserted. The wind picks up, an empty cigarette pack skittering across the road.

"Sure," I say nervously. This close to Mason, I'm aware of how much bigger he is than me. His chest muscles strain against his work T-shirt and his arms are thick and ropey.

"What was that today?" Mason says, taking off his baseball cap and rubbing the top of his head. "Your dropping by unannounced? I thought you knew you should call first."

"Sometimes I just need to see Jenna."

Mason slaps his cap against his thigh. "I'm real worried about her. She's been so stressed lately, and you're not helping. Dissing our relationship, telling her she can't trust me—you're not acting like a friend. Not like the sister I know you are."

She told him what I said. Heat fills my cheeks like he's slapped me. "I just want her to be happy and safe," I say.

"She is with me," he says. "More than she ever was with your self-absorbed family."

That's a lie. My parents never hurt Jenna or me, not intentionally, and not the way he's hurting her. Though I know she hurts from feeling like Mom abandoned her for me.

Mason's eyes look pained and he keeps shifting from foot to foot, like he's uncomfortable with what he's saying. He doesn't look like a man who beats his wife.

"Look, I know you love her," he says, "But sometimes we don't see what we're doing to the people who're closest to us. I've come to ask you to stop hurting her."

My cheeks sting. "I'm not the one who's hurting her." Am I?

"I love Jenna. I'd never do anything to hurt her," Mason says. "She's the best thing in my life! But you—you came over trying to stir up trouble between us, trying to make her doubt me."

I bite my lip. I never actually saw him hit Jenna—except in my mind's eye.

He steps closer. "You sent that email about the Audi, didn't you? Lying to my face? What was your end game?"

"I—I just wanted to talk to Jenna alone, the way we used to."

Mason snorts. "You never had that kind of relationship. You still don't." He leans in. "Do you know how alone she felt in your house, Kate? How unloved and ignored?" His face and neck are a mottled red. "I'm the only one who loves her the way she should be loved. Who sees her for who she is."

I think my dad does. And I love her, too. "She seems so unhappy."

"That's what I'm trying to tell you!" Mason slaps his cap against his thigh again. "You're making her doubt the only good thing she's ever had. The only person who's truly hers."

It feels surreal to be standing here having this conversation, when he tried to kill Jenna only a few hours ago. But I didn't actually see it happen. And Mason looks so concerned for her. Maybe I really *am* hallucinating it all.

But my visions feel so real. And I was right about Inez. And the others.

"Will you stop lying to Jenna?" Mason asks, sounding hopeful.

I can't promise that. Not if my visions are real. But are they? "I promise I'm trying to look out for her," I say.

"That's what I'm trying to do," Mason says bitterly, running his hand through his hair.

But I don't know if I can believe him.

26

MASON AND JENNA ARRIVE at our house together, as if Mason hadn't been waiting for me only an hour earlier. Jenna's smile is too bright and brittle, and she's moving a little too carefully. She's wearing a silk scarf tied around her neck. To hide a bruise? But she's alive. I breathe in easier.

Mason hovers next to her, like he needs to breathe in her air to exist. His hair is combed back, his hands scrubbed, he's switched his T-shirt for a dress shirt, and he stinks of mouthwash—to cover up his smoking. Mom and Dad watch them, trying not to look like they are.

"It smells good in here," Jenna says cheerfully. "I know it's vegetarian," she glances at me, "But what is it?"

Another thing to resent me for—Mom going vegetarian for my health.

"Quiche, salad, and squash soup," Mom says. "Hope you like those, Mason."

"Oh, I'll eat anything, ma'am," Mason says, smiling an aw-shucks smile.

"Good man," Dad says, clapping Mason on the shoulder. "That's the right answer."

"I brought French bread from the bakery," Jenna says, handing Mom the crinkly paper bag.

"That's perfect," Mom says. "But you didn't have to bring anything!"

"I wanted to."

"I'm glad you came," I say, moving closer to Jenna. "How're you doing?"

"Jenna's just fine," Mason says, pulling Jenna to him. Jenna smiles brightly. "In fact, she's more than fine. She's pregnant!"

"Jenna!" Mom cries, shoving the bread at Dad and rushing to hug Jenna.

Dad's face gets all red and he pumps Mason's hand up and down, then hugs Jenna like she's a delicate flower he might crush.

"Congratulations," I say, hugging her gently. Thoughts whirl through my head like shards of glass in a tornado. If Mason is beating her now, what's he going to do when the baby's born? A wailing, attention-demanding baby? Is her pregnancy why she thinks everything will get better? And is that why Mason almost killed her today? Because she's pregnant?

"That's just—incredible!" I force a smile.

"I was going to tell you myself," Jenna says, squeezing my arm. "But we wanted to wait to tell you all together. Are you happy for me?"

"Of course I am," I say. "Wow—I can't believe I'll be an aunt!" But how can she stay with him now?

"I would've made something special if I'd known," Mom says, wringing her hands.

"It's fine, Mom. Whatever you made is great," Jenna says.

"I'll get some sparkling cranberry juice from the fridge to celebrate," Dad says, striding out of the room, still carrying the bread.

"How far along are you?" Mom asks, resting her hand on Jenna's belly.

"Just twelve weeks." Jenna puts her hand protectively over her stomach. "I—we wanted to wait until I passed that point to tell you.

I waited to tell everyone, in case..." Her voice trails off.

"You remember my miscarriages?" Mom asks quietly.

Miscarriages? I stare at her. "I never knew."

Mom twists her ring around her finger. "Most miscarriages happen in the first three months of pregnancy. I had two. I didn't want you to know because you were so young—"

I frown. I wasn't much younger than Jenna.

"And sick," Mom says. She turns back to Jenna. "But you've passed that point? I'm so glad for you, honey. For you both." Her voice is full of tears.

Jenna's been pregnant for three months. And if my visions are real, Mason kicked her in the stomach while she was pregnant—never mind that he tried to kill her. It's amazing she *didn't* have a miscarriage. I grit my teeth, wishing I could get her away from him and somewhere safe.

"Have you told Asha and Rina yet?" I ask. Maybe her friends can talk some sense into her.

"You're the first ones we've told, aside from my mom," Mason says, resting his hand on the back of Jenna's neck. "We saw her earlier today."

"I've kind of drifted apart from my friends," Jenna says. "We don't have that much in common anymore."

"Oh, you'll have to call them and tell them your news!" Mom says. "They'll be so happy for you!"

"*I'm* happy for her—enough to light up the world," Mason says, puffing out his chest.

"I know you are." Mom pats his hand. "As are we. Now come along, everyone! Let's eat."

Mom leads the way into the dining room. She's put cloth napkins out on the table, the way she does for company, and a bowl of salad. Dad dropped the French bread in the center. Mason pulls out Jenna's chair for her and she looks up at him gratefully, like he just did something wonderful. I try not to roll my eyes.

Dad comes in with a tray of wine glasses of sparkling cranberry juice, giving one to each of us, even though I hate carbonated anything.

"To Jenna and Mason's pregnancy!" Dad cries, raising his glass high. "To a healthy, happy baby!"

We all raise our glasses and drink. I sip reluctantly. A baby should be something to celebrate, but how can it be a celebration when they're bringing a baby into a home full of violence and abuse?

"Kate, help me get the food from the kitchen," Mom says. I follow her in, taking the quiche out of the oven where it was warming, while Mom pours the soup into a big tureen. Dad and Mason's laughter rumbles from the living room.

"Do you really think she's okay?" I ask Mom quietly.

"Not now," she whispers, plastering on a wide smile, picking up the tureen. We head back out to the living room, setting the dishes on the table. "Dig in, everyone!"

I sit at my place. Mason leans over and whispers something to Jenna and she laughs, her laughter sounding too bright and fake, her smile like plastic.

My stomach clenches. It's going to be so much harder for her to escape once she's had the baby. I wonder if she's thought of that, and of protecting this new life. Or if she's just caught up in fear or denial.

Mason's sitting across from me. He and Dad talk animatedly about football and cars as they eat. Mom and Jenna talk about the new baby, a baby shower, a sleep schedule. I don't know how Mom or Dad's going to get any time to talk to Jenna alone. Mason is hyper focused on Jenna, always getting her anything she might want before she even asks. The perfect attentive husband—only he's not.

Soon Mom starts clearing the dishes. Jenna gets up to help her and I'm relieved—maybe they'll have a minute to talk now. But then Mason jumps up, taking his glass and Dad's, and joins them in the kitchen.

I scowl after him.

"Be happy for Jenna, Kate," Dad says. "She's starting a family."

How can I be happy for her if she's in danger?

Mason, Jenna, and Mom come back carrying bowls of apple crumble.

Just as I'm spooning up a piece of the sweet apple, brown sugar, and oats, Mason clears his throat.

"This is real hard to say, but I don't know how else to do this except to just say it." He points his spoon at me, and looks at my dad. "Do you know your daughter thinks she sees visions? And that she can predict the future?"

I'm sitting right here, jerk.

Mom freezes, her spoon midair. Dad pauses, mid-chew.

"Yes. Yes, we do," Mom says.

"Have you considered that maybe there's something medically wrong with her?" Mason leans forward. Outside, thunder rumbles. "Jenna says she only gets these 'visions,'" He makes air quotes with his fingers, "When she has an asthma attack. Maybe it's hypoxia."

I stiffen. That's what the doctor told Mason in my vision. "Really?" I say. "That's what you're going with?"

Mason shakes his head, his gaze focused on my dad. "Hallucinations can also come from mental illness. I wouldn't be bringing this up, but there's things she's been saying lately about us that upset Jenna and it's got me worried. Don't you think you should get Kate checked out? Get her treated if she needs help?"

My body grows cold. He's trying to discredit me, throw suspicion off him.

Jenna bows her head, her hair hiding her face.

"It's not your place to tell us how to raise our daughter," Dad says, his cheeks and face flushed, wagging his spoon at Mason so hard a piece of apple drops onto the tablecloth.

I'm surprised he didn't just agree with him.

Mason leans forward, rapping the table. "I'm sorry, sir, but I disagree. When her behavior hurts my wife, it's my business." He turns to me. "I've arranged an appointment with a specialist. If you'd just see him—"

I can hardly believe this is happening. "No," I say. I look at Jenna. *Say something!*

Jenna raises her head. "You should go see the doctor," she says softly, her eyes pleading with me. "What can it hurt?"

Has she forgotten all those months after the police and social workers invaded our home? Mom and Dad's sadness, their anger, their silence? The way they barely looked at me? I haven't. "I don't have mental health issues," I say, my voice shaking. "Not ones that make me hallucinate. I told you—I'm not hallucinating or lying."

"It could be medical," Mason says smoothly, "Something completely out of your control. But it should be looked at—if only for your health. You may need treatment or medication to get healthy."

Right. Play the health card. I glance at Mom. Her face is still and tight, her eyes darting back and forth between us, her eyes full of worry.

"That's enough!" Dad rams his chair back and stands. "Who do you think you are to come here and tell us how to raise our daughter?" he shouts. "Kate is just fine!" He avoids looking at me. Mason's clearly sown doubt in Dad about me. In Mom, too. Doubt they already had, but probably hadn't labelled so clearly.

"Ian," Mom says, tugging his arm, "Sit down."

"I disagree, sir," Mason says, leaning back in his chair like he owns the place. "Hallucinations, lies, whatever this is, aren't something to ignore. She's causing Jenna a lot of pain. And if it's something that can be treated, why not treat the source of the problem?"

Oh, that's rich. *I'm* the problem. I glance over at Jenna. Her head is bowed, her hands clenched in her lap.

"Jenna, tell him I'm not hallucinating or lying," I say. "You know I didn't make it up."

Jenna raises her head, her eyes brimming over. Her gaze darts to

Mason, then back to me.

"She can't tell you that," Mason says, "Because it's not true."

"I wasn't asking you. I was asking Jenna," I say. "Jenna?"

Jenna shakes her head, her eyes pleading. "You *have* to stop your accusations." A tear slides down her cheek. "It's not fair to Mason and me."

"There. You see how hard this is on Jenna?" Mason asks.

Outside, lightning cracks, and I jump. Rain beats against the windows.

"She made Jenna cry again." Mason stands, knocking over his wine glass, red staining the tablecloth in a widening pool. "You need to get your daughter under control." He grips Jenna's shoulder. "Come on, babe. Let's go home." He holds out his hand.

Jenna lets him help her up and leans into him, like he's sheltering her from a bully.

Mom stands, too, her twisted napkin in her hand. "Please don't go, Jenna. Mason. I know you're upset, but let's try to work this out. We love you."

"You have a funny way of showing your love," Mason says, guiding Jenna out of the living room, his arm around her. "You play favorites and Jenna's always come last. Why should I be surprised it's no different now?"

His words punch my gut.

"That's not true," Mom says, trailing after them, but Jenna and Mason are already out the door, rain striking the floor in the entranceway. "Drive safe!" she yells, but I doubt they heard her over the howling wind and rain. She stands there for a moment, looking out into the darkness, then shuts the door.

Mom walks back in, the front of her dress wet in big splotches, and plunks herself onto her chair, staring vacantly at the table. "What just happened?"

Dad sits, then rubs his face with his hands. "I shouldn't have lost my temper. But that boy—I've never liked him. And Jenna's withdrawn since she's been with him." Dad sighs heavily, and looks at me. "I don't know what's right to do here. I want to do what's right for both Jenna and you. Maybe we've let this vision nonsense go on too long—"

"They're real!" I say.

Dad holds up his hand. "I know you believe they are. But I think there's a simpler explanation. Maybe it's just that you have a good sense of people, and strong observation skills. Tell us what you 'saw' again."

I swallow tightly. If I tell them again will they lean towards Mason's theory that I'm hallucinating? Or will they listen to me?

I crease my napkin in my hands, folding and refolding it, and tell them about the photo, the shattered glass, the beating that I saw in my visions. And again about Mason killing her, even though he didn't mean to.

Dad sits there quietly, his eyes dark, his jaw clenched, his hands clasped so tightly in front of him that the tips of his fingers are white. Mom's face looks almost bloodless, her eyes glassy with tears.

"I don't know how you come to these visions of yours," Dad says once I finish, "But I suspect it's a combination of your gut instincts and your reading body language. Jenna looked miserable tonight, maybe even trapped by her pregnancy. Still, Mason may have a good point—that we should at least make an appointment with a professional for you. Elizabeth, what do you think?"

My stomach tightens.

"I think we're losing Jenna," Mom says in a warbly voice, propping her head up with her hands. "I never played favorites—but Kate's health took up more of my attention and time, and Mason's playing on that. She didn't even try to talk to us alone, but she might've if Mason hadn't been with her every second of the night. And I don't like what he said about Kate, or how he said it. I'm worried about Jenna, Ian. Something's not right there."

I told you what's not right! I want to say, but I don't. That they're even considering that there might be truth to my visions amazes me, even if they don't believe how I see them. And the most important thing is that we protect Jenna. But I hope they don't send me to a psychiatrist, try to label and medicate me. I have issues like most everyone, but I don't hallucinate.

"What do we do?" I say. "Jenna won't admit he's hitting her. How do we get her safe?"

"Jenna and I haven't spent much time together since she eloped," Mom says. "Mason always comes with her or unexpectedly drops by. I think it's time I took her out for lunch on her own. Maybe she'll talk to me then."

"I could invite Mason out for a beer at the same time," Dad says. "Make sure he doesn't try to invade your time with her."

"So you'll ask her out right away?" I press. "For tomorrow?"

"Yes. I'll tell her I want to plan a baby shower for her."

I think about the way Jenna leaned into Mason, like he was protecting her from us—from me. "What if you can't get her to tell you anything?"

Mom massages her forehead. "I'm not going to let a child of mine get hurt. I need to hear it from Jenna herself—but if I find out that Mason has been beating her, I will do serious bodily damage to that man, and that's a promise."

She stands and gathers dishes to take into the kitchen. They clatter in her hands.

I jump up to help and Dad does, too. We clear the table silently, until all that's left is the big red stain on the tablecloth like blood.

27

I LIE ON MY bed, staring up at my ceiling. I can't get Jenna's face out of my head, the way her eyes pleaded with me. I know she's hurting. Everyone can see that. But what if I'm wrong about why? What if Mason's not the one who's hurting her? What if it is me, seeing something that's not real?

My cell rings. Jenna. I take a deep breath and answer.

"You need to back off," Jenna says, her voice thick. "Mason's becoming obsessive about you and the way you're trying to break us up. He begged me not to leave him. I've never seen him like this. Whatever you think you saw, Kate, you have to stop talking about it."

"I'm just trying to help you," I say.

"You want to help me?" Jenna says. "You really want to help? Then stop accusing Mason of hurting me! Stop telling everyone. Just stop, okay?" Her voice shakes. "You're making it worse."

"Why don't you come stay with us for a few days?"

"Kate!" Jenna shouts, her voice cracking. "I mean it. Mom and Dad may let you do anything you want, but I won't. Just stop!"

And she hangs up.

I growl, wanting to throw my phone across the room. Instead, I flick open Letter Quest and tap out words, trying to calm myself. I never saw my visions as a curse, but they're starting to feel like one.

Or maybe it's how I'm using them. Maybe I shouldn't tell anyone about them. But how can I let Jenna keep getting beaten? At least Inez was helped by my visions, wasn't she?

I text Desi. They don't respond.

I tap out word after word, defeating monsters, going through levels I've already gone through. I close the game and open up Wow Word, wanting the encouragement of the bookworm.

My phone vibrates. I tap the text notification.

Can't talk now. More later.

This time I really do throw my cell across the room.

Saturday morning everything feels better. We got through Friday—and Jenna and Inez are both still alive. Desi and Nana were right, after all. We really can change what I see. I feel like I can breathe easier, think better, like a slab of concrete has been lifted off my chest.

I eat my organic oatmeal and raspberries with enthusiasm.

The doorbell rings. "I'll get it," Mom says, setting down her coffee mug.

Voices murmur, then Mom calls "Kate, it's for you!"

Nobody ever comes to see me. I walk out to find Mom standing in the doorway beside Desi, a bemused look on her face.

"Oh! Mom, this is Desi. Desi, this is my mom," I say.

"Yes, we've met," Mom says dryly.

Desi shuffles their feet. "I thought maybe we could go to the library for their paper-bag book-making class, then a used bookstore, then a meal. Spend half the day together." They look at my mom. "That is, if that's okay with you, Mrs. Robbins."

I grin at them so widely my cheeks hurt.

"It is if it's okay with Kate."

"I'll be right there!" I say. I race to the bathroom to brush my teeth and fix my hair, then grab my backpack. I turn to find Mom right behind me.

"Did you take your medication? What was your peak flow like?"

So much for not hounding me about my asthma. "Yes. The usual. And I've got my inhaler; I always do. Did Jenna say yes to getting together?"

"Yes," Mom says, twisting her ring. "She sounded excited about the baby shower. We're on for this afternoon." She brushes my hair out of my face. "So Desi's taking you on a date."

My face burns. "Yeah."

Mom smiles. "You two look cute together."

"Gotta go. Bye, Mom!" I run down the stairs and head out the door before she can say anything else.

The sun shines bright in the blue sky, Desi close beside me. I bounce as I walk. I don't even notice the car exhaust, or care about the woman passing us with such strong perfume it clogs my throat.

"I can't believe you thought of this!" I say, kissing Desi on the cheek. "You're so sweet."

Desi shrugs, but they're grinning. "It's past the D Day for both our sisters, so I figured we could focus on us for a while."

"We've still got to watch them," I say. "Just because they passed the date in my visions doesn't mean everything's okay."

"Believe me, I know," Desi says, shoving their fingers through their hair. "Inez is still dealing with suicidal thoughts and depression from the trauma, and Jenna must still be being abused. But you and I worked hard. We deserve some time off just for ourselves."

I look at them closer. They have dark circles beneath their eyes. They need a break from all the stress as much as I do. "Are you okay?" I ask. "I know it's been tough with Inez. And it was a lot to learn about your mom."

"It was." Desi looks at me grimly. "Sorry I couldn't talk last night. Inez was sobbing about wanting to die, but she couldn't bear to hurt Nana and me. It was a long night. I wish I could kill the bastards who raped her. And her ex for posting that nude."

I reach for their hand. "I'm so sorry."

"Nana made a big jug of chilate and we sat on Inez's bed with her, holding her while she cried. She was pretty wrung out, and she still won't see a counselor or even call a crisis line. But at least she hasn't acted on it. I have you to thank for that." They squeeze my hand. "How's Jenna?"

"Pregnant," I say.

"Mierda!" Desi says. "That'll trap her."

"Exactly. She's so unhappy, but she won't admit anything's going on. And then she acted like Mason's the one who's protecting her from me. She said I'm hurting her. I don't know. Maybe my visions only make things worse."

"You can't really believe that," Desi says, their hand tightening on mine. "If you hadn't told me about Inez, she might've actually—" Desi's voice chokes off. "Seriously, Kate—I will be forever grateful to you."

My chest tightens. I look away, staring at the grimy, cracked sidewalk, a broken glass bottle, the green shards glinting in the sun. I kick at a piece and it skitters across the concrete.

"What's wrong?" Desi asks.

"It's stupid."

"No, tell me."

I shrug. "I don't want you to like me because you feel grateful. I want you to like me for me."

"I do!" Desi stops, grabbing my arms. "You must know that's not why I'm with you. I was drawn to you the first time I saw you reading a queer book in class without Mrs. Levi seeing it. I think it was... *The Athena Protocol*?"

"That was last year!" I say, laughing.

"I know. I told you I've been thinking about you for a long time. And I was even more drawn to you when you gave it to Jada after her father died. I like being near you. I feel good around you."

"Really?" I stare into their warm brown eyes.

"Yes, Cielo. There's something special about you—your kindness and determination. You make me feel like I can't give up because you don't. You have a strength about you," they say, their thumb rubbing my cheek. "Even though you also have a softness, a vulnerability. I love that about you." They lean in and kiss me.

I kiss them back, their lips soft and full, their strong arms holding me tight. I feel more cherished and loved than I have in a long time. More seen. No one's ever seen my strength or determination before, or liked my softness. The way I care too much. But Desi's got a lot of that in them, too. They have so much compassion.

I break the kiss and grin at them. "It's a perfect day," I say, grabbing their hand. We start walking again, heading towards the library. I wonder what queer books we'll find, what adventures we'll have. I grin at Desi again, only to find them frowning. "What's wrong?"

"I'm sorry—I was just worrying about Inez. I told myself I wouldn't today."

"I get it. You were up with her in the night. Maybe we should go back and check on her."

"No!" Desi says. "This is our day."

But they don't look any less worried. And I feel guilty that I'd been so happy with Desi when Inez is still suffering, and Jenna must be so scared now that she's pregnant. Even as we walk, Mason could be beating her again, and I know she's not going to tell anyone. It's not just Jenna and Inez I have to protect now; it's Jenna's baby, too.

What if we haven't done enough for Jenna and Inez? What if Inez still tries to kill herself? Or Mason still kills Jenna?

"I'm sorry; I spoiled the mood," Desi says.

"No, it's okay," I say. "I'd rather know what's going on for you." And I should know what's going on with Jenna and Inez.

How can I know if we've thwarted the worst for our sisters if I don't have another vision? I can't just wait for one to happen. Who knows when that will be? It could be too late.

On an impulse, I let go of Desi's hand and shout, "Race you to the library!"

I run off down the street past empty houses, then a bus shelter, the sidewalk littered with cigarette butts. Ahead of me a mother pushes her stroller, a car backs out of a driveway, an old woman bends down to pat a cat.

"Kate, wait!" Desi shouts, running after me.

My wheezing gets louder, my breath shorter. My chest hurts with every breath.

Desi grabs my arm, yanking me back. "What was that? You shouldn't be running, should you?"

They're too late. I bend over, coughing as my lungs narrow. Houses stare out at me with vacant eyes.

Desi fumbles with my backpack, unzipping the front pocket. I need the vision to come. I force another cough. My sight shifts, the world around me growing fuzzy, and instead of fighting it, I relax my eyes.

Mason pumps gas for a customer, listening on his wireless earbuds as I call Jenna. He hears me asking if he's ever hurt her, if I can come over. "Badmouthing me," Mason mutters. He finishes with the customer and yanks out his cell, opening up his spyware. He clicks on the GPS option. "Yep. Jenna's still at home."

"Excuse me?" a customer says.

"Nothing," Mason says. "Just talking to myself."

Desi shoves my inhaler into my hand. My chest aches, my heart pounds too hard. I want to see more, need to, but I'm struggling for air. I suck in the medicine, holding it in my lungs as long as I can before I start coughing again, my legs so weak I fall to my knees. Desi holds me up, pushing the inhaler into my mouth. I use it again.

"Is she okay?" a woman asks, stopping beside us, a bag of groceries in her hand. "Should I call an ambulance?"

"I don't know! Her inhaler's supposed to help. Let's give it a minute to work," Desi says. "She lives just a few blocks away."

"I'm fine," I croak out, and wave the woman on.

The woman watches me with doubtful eyes but she leaves, looking once over her shoulder at us.

Mason calls a buddy to cover him, grabs a candy bar from the candy display, flowers from the bucket near the door, then jumps into his car. He drives through red lights, tires screeching, listening in as Jenna and I talk in the kitchen. "Jenna's bitch sister thinks she can fill her head with lies? I'll shut her up, get her diagnosed with something that'll keep anyone from believing her. And Jenna just lets her lie? What kind of loyalty is that? After all I've done for her. Just wait 'til I deal with her."

He wrenches open the apartment door, fixes a smile on his face, and makes nice with Jenna until Kate leaves. Then he beats Jenna where no one will see it, kicking her ribs and back until she doesn't even cry out any more. He drags her into the bedroom.

Oh god. I cough, straining for air. Did I make things worse, trying to help Jenna? But I can't ignore what's happened to her. I cough harder.

"I'm calling nine-one-one," Desi says, pulling out their cell.

I grab their arm. "No." I cough. "Getting better." I suck on my inhaler again, willing the medicine to work.

"Kate," Desi says, their voice tight.

I shake my head, gasping, and hold up a finger. "Give me...a minute." My chest loosens up a little.

I cough again and drag in more air. "He's spying on Jenna." I cough.

Desi crouches down in front of me. "Who? Mason?"

I nod and cough some more. Use the inhaler again. No way am I going to the hospital. "Spies on her, then hurts her." I cough again.

"Always have your cell on you!" Mason roars. "I've gotta be able to reach you any time I need you."

Jenna cringes, nodding.

Mason smiles, fingering the cell in his jeans pocket.

"I'm taking you home," Desi says.

"No. It's almost over," I say. "We have to help Jenna."

"Yeah, we do. But not like this."

28

I LOOK UP AT Desi, my chest tightening. I cough again, then suck more air into my whistling lungs. "Like what?"

Desi stands and pulls me up with them. Their face is dark, their mouth tight. "You did this on purpose. You triggered an attack to get a vision."

Crap. I didn't think they'd know. "I have to help our sisters." I cough harder, my chest tightening again.

Inez strides home from school, repeatedly looking over her shoulder. Three teen boys follow her, their school blazers flapping. "Slut!" they shout.

They drag her into an alley and ram her up against the wall. Inez punches and kicks them, but there are too many and they are too strong.

"Get off me!" Inez shouts. "Help, somebody help!"

One guy pins her by the neck with his arm, throttling her voice, while he unzips her pants. "You know you want it. You can't just tease us and then refuse. Mikka told us how much you like it rough." The boy laughs. "I never would've thought it from the ice queen."

"No, stop!" Inez cries, her voice strangled. "This is rape."

The boy sneers. "I've seen your pics. That's consent enough."

Inez screams, punching at him.

"Kate!" Desi pushes my inhaler toward my mouth. "If this doesn't get better fast I don't care what you say, I'm calling nine one one."

"It's getting better!" I say, wheezing, and cough again.

Inez rocks on her bed, arms wrapped tight around her stomach. "No one will believe me," she whispers to herself. "The girl who posed nude and then cried rape. Who asked for it." Tears stream down her reddened cheeks. "Three upstanding boys against slutty bi old me." She snuffles. "They didn't do anything to Mikka when he posted the pics; just shamed me. They won't do anything to these guys." She gets up, lifts up her mattress, and pulls out a stash of hidden pills.

"Don't you want to know what I saw about Inez?" I cough again, my chest aching but my breath is coming easier, now.

"You know I do!" Desi yells, their eyes too bright. "But you can't keep doing this. How is it going to help Inez and Jenna if you die trying to see a vision? Do you know how guilty they'll feel?"

"They won't know! And I'm not going to die."

"*I'll* know!" Desi jabs their chest. "And you don't know you won't!"

In the house across the street, someone pulls back the drapes and a face appears at the window.

"I'm sorry," I say. "I didn't know how else to help." I wheeze harder.

"Nana told you how!" Desi shouts. "Practice what she taught you!"

"I only get flickers that way."

"Then practice harder! It's not worth your life!"

I nod to show I heard them.

I have to stay calm. I can talk in complete sentences again, which means I'm out of the danger zone. But strong emotion can trigger another attack, or make this one worse. I breathe out. "Inez was raped by three boys from school," I gasp-cough. "They said her ex

Mikka told them she liked it rough. And that her nude pics were consent."

Desi's hands clench. "The bastards! Tell me who they are! I'll kill them all!" A vein in their neck pulses.

I've never seen them so angry. It should frighten me, after seeing what Mason's done to Jenna, but it doesn't feel the same. This is protective rage. "I didn't recognize them; I only know they're from school because of their jackets."

"Can you pick them out of the yearbooks?" Desi asks hoarsely.

"I don't know," I say, a wheeze in my voice. "But even if I could, that's up to Inez, not me. And I don't think she's ready for that."

"Mierda!" Desi slumps. "Maybe what you told me will help me help her. But neither Inez or Jenna would want you to kill yourself just to help them!" The vein in Desi's neck is pulsing again. "Was all that stuff you told Inez about wanting to live just a lie?"

"Of course not," I say. "I'm not trying to...to hurt myself."

Desi sucks in a breath, their eyes welling. "You could've fooled me. You have to care more about yourself than this! You have to protect your own health."

I swallow, my throat full of tears. "I know," I say, and cough.

"Then start acting like it!" Desi yells. "Don't hurt yourself like this again."

"I have to try to help them if I can! If you could see what Mason's done to Jenna—"

"So you call the police." Desi jerks their hands towards the sky, their whole body tense. "You don't try to stop it yourself. And you don't risk your life by sparking an asthma attack. I like you, Kate; I like you a lot. But I won't watch you hurt yourself."

"Then don't watch," I say, wheezing.

"All right, I won't!" Desi scowls, then spins around and stalks away.

So much for our dream date.

The sky is grey with roiling clouds—exactly the way I feel. I walk to the library alone, still wheezing.

All through the craft-making class at the library, I think Desi will text or call—but they don't. They must still be furious at me. But my forcing an attack got me the info we need to help our sisters more—even though it didn't tell me if they're still in danger.

I stab at the brown paper bag with my pen. Maybe since I didn't see anything from the future, that means they're not in danger anymore? I wish I knew if that's true.

But I found out important things that I wouldn't have known otherwise. I know more about why Inez wants to kill herself. Maybe it'll help her heal if she talks about it. And I found out that Mason's spying on Jenna through her cell. That's why he came home early when I was at her place. That's how he knows what I've been saying to her. And that's why he's been beating her even more—because of our conversations.

My throat feels too tight, my eyes hot. I see Jenna again on the floor, curled up against the pain. She could lose the baby. Sustain internal injuries. Get a concussion. Die. And I made it worse by telling her what I know while Mason listened in.

I chew on my lip so hard it brings tears to my eyes. I have to find a way to get Jenna out of there—without her phone.

I wish Desi would call or text, but I know I scared them. I pull out my cell and text them. **I'm sorry I scared you. You're right; it was risky.**

I wait, but there are no moving dots showing they're texting, so I go back to my paper-bag book—a list of all the things I like about them. I hope I'll be able to give it to them. I hope we're still together.

I finish up my paper-bag book, stuff it into my backpack, and leave the library, checking my cell. Still nothing from Desi. I look up and down the street, hoping to see their familiar face, but they're not here.

I decide to go on the rest of our "date" by myself, determined to have a good time—and hoping they'll show up, even though they won't know where I am. I don't want to go home early and have to explain to Mom that our date ended because I forced an asthma attack.

I grab a sandwich and a bottle of water from a local bagel shop, eating in the park, the sky growing darker, then head to the used bookstore, but it's hard to focus on anything but Desi. I buy a book for Desi with a nonbinary character—*Sir Callie And the Champions of Helston*—and stuff it into my backpack.

I trudge out of the bookshop, my body heavy and sluggish, like it's full of mud. Triggering visions wasn't worth wrecking my relationship. But can I promise not to do it again—and mean it?

I text something easier: **You were right. I need to practice what your nana taught me more.**

Still no response.

I start toward home.

My phone shrills. I yank my cell out of my pocket, hoping it's Desi. "Jenna?"

"You bitch, how could you do this to me? I told you to back off!"

"What're you talking about?" I ask.

"You phoned the cops on Mason!"

"What?" I stop walking. "No, I didn't. I swear I didn't." My mind races. Who could've done this? A neighbor? But Jenna barely made a sound when Mason beat her. Mom and Dad? But they would've talked to me first.

"Don't lie to me. Mom and Dad would never do this." Jenna's screaming and crying, her voice breaking up. "I won't press charges against him, do you hear me? I'm going to bail him out, and he'll be back home with me where he belongs. And Mason? He'll never forgive you. You have no idea how long he can hold a grudge. You've gone too far, Kate. Crossed a line and done something you can't take back."

"I didn't do it, Jenna; I swear!" I cry. "You know I wouldn't!"

But Desi might. Desi, who's been telling me to call the cops. Who didn't want me to trigger my visions. Who hasn't texted or called me back. My feet grow heavy.

"I don't know anything anymore, not when it comes to you," Jenna says. "I'm scared for you, Kate; I really am." Her voice breaks. "Mason swore he'd get even with you. I've never seen him so enraged. You're out of my life. For good!" The phone goes dead.

I stop walking and stare at my cell, blinking back tears. Jenna's cut me out of her life like I'm some malignant growth, like I've harmed her instead of trying to help her. And Desi isn't talking to me, either. I swipe at my eyes. Have I really hurt them that badly? Am I the problem?

Dark clouds cover the sun, the air growing heavy.

My chest feels like it's caving inward, my flesh disintegrating, filling up my lungs. Two people I love are telling me I am. Sure makes it likely. My stomach heaves, like I might vomit.

I swallow hard, then call Desi.

Their phone rings multiple times, then goes to voicemail. I call again and again, leaning up against a building that smells faintly of urine, my legs barely holding me up. People stride past me.

"Hello?" Desi says, sounding cautious.

"Did you call the cops on Mason?" I ask, trembling.

"Somebody had to."

I can't believe they did that. "How could you betray me like this?"

"Betray you?" Desi's voice cracks. "I'm trying to protect you. To save your life!" they shout.

I bump my head back lightly against the brick wall. "I didn't ask you to!"

"I couldn't just stand by and watch you risk your life when there are other ways to protect your sister," Desi says.

"Yeah. Ways that infuriate a man who's good with his fists!" I grit my teeth. "You probably made him want to beat Jenna more! And me too, because he'll assume it was me."

There's a tense silence. "I hadn't thought of that. I'm sorry," Desi says, their voice heavy. "I tried to be careful, said I was a neighbor who heard the screams. I got Inez to call, too. I didn't think Jenna'd know." Desi sighs. "I'll fix it. I'll tell her it was me. She'll tell Mason, and he won't blame you."

"That won't fix anything!" I yell. "There's no way you could've known what was happening if I hadn't told you." People stare at me as they walk past, but I'm too upset to care. "It all comes back to me."

"Maybe I didn't do things the way you wanted me to," Desi shouts, "But I did my best to protect you and Jenna both. It's better than you killing yourself with an asthma attack to help her."

"Desi—" I say.

"No, I told you; I can't watch you do this to yourself. I won't." They hang up.

I stare at my phone. Did they just break up with me?

I call them back over and over again, but they don't pick up.

29

THE DARK CLOUDS BURST open, cold rain pelting down, soaking me to the skin. I trudge down the street, my socks squishing in my shoes. I can't believe everything is such a mess. Desi broke up with me, even though they acted behind my back and made things worse. Jenna's cut me out of her life. She and Inez are still in danger. And Mason blames me.

He'll take it out on Jenna. She's in more danger now, not less. And then he'll come after me, convince my parents that I've got mental health issues that make me hallucinate, get them to medicate me, maybe even lock me up in some secure ward. They were already half believing his lies. Or maybe he'll try to physically hurt me the way he does Jenna. But manipulation and lies seem more his tactic unless he can get hold of me in private—and there's no way I'm going anywhere near Mason alone.

The rain strikes at me skin, my face, mixing with my tears. I want to scream at the sky. Is this how my trying to change my visions is going to end—with everyone hating me, and Jenna and Inez dying any way?

I swipe the rain from my eyes and stomp through a puddle, water chilling my feet.

I don't know how to fix anything. I've only made things worse. Maybe I should just go back to ignoring my visions. Agree that Desi and I are better off broken up.

My heart aches like a rib bone has pierced it, slicing it open from all this unnecessary drama. If I'd just kept my mouth shut, Desi and I wouldn't have gotten close. Inez and Jenna would die any way, but I wouldn't have put everyone else through all this pain. I wish I'd never listened to my visions.

No, I wish I'd done better with the information I had. The cold rain beats at me harder, little pebbles of water stinging my skin, and I welcome the pain.

I should have found a way to convince Jenna of my visions. Maybe told her about Inez being in danger, too. Or reminded her of all the times I was right.

Desi's angry, brittle voice reverberates through my mind. I should've listened to Desi and their nana, should've practiced the techniques Nana taught me every free moment until I'd found a way to bring on the visions without hurting myself. If I had, I wouldn't have lost the human I love. Because I do love them; I know that now.

Tears burst out of me in loud, wracking sobs, almost drowned out by the pouring rain and the traffic rushing by.

I hope I get another chance with Desi. With Jenna, too.

Desi's the only person I've ever felt truly sees me and likes what they see. They make me feel more alive, like I want to live every day instead of feeling like the day is just something to get through chronically ill, alone, with no one believing what I see. Their hope and warmth makes me more hopeful. I don't want to lose them. I can't. It'd be like learning I could experience joy to going back to just existing.

My throat is raw, my entire body cold. A car races by, splashing me with a giant puddle of dirty rain water. I trudge forward.

How could I have ignored Desi's limits? Not listened to them when they said they couldn't watch me risk my life? If our positions were reversed, would I really be able to watch them put their life repeatedly at risk when I knew there was another way?

I clench my teeth. I'd be furious at them—furious and terrified and sad—because they matter too much to me. Because their life has meaning. And so does mine, just as much as the people we're trying to save.

I stomp through another puddle, stomp so hard the cement jolts my bones. My parents may not understand me, even Jenna doesn't, but I know they love me in their own way. And it'd hurt them if I died trying to save Jenna. Or worse, if we both died.

I thought I was being selfless, but I was actually being selfish. Repeatedly putting myself in danger to help someone when I could've protected both of us is a shit move. No wonder Desi stopped talking to me. No wonder they broke it off when I was breaking their heart over and over again.

The rain eases, the drops lighter now, softer. I reach the end of my street, light pouring from our windows.

I need to fix things. I need to beg Desi for forgiveness. I need to practice Nana's techniques. Convince Jenna I'm telling the truth. Figure out what else I need to say to Inez. And get my parents to believe me.

MOM'S WAITING FOR ME in the doorway with a towel, her face lined with worry. "How's your asthma?"

"It's fine," I say, rubbing my hair with the towel, and trying to keep from dripping on the floor.

Mom leans in closer.

I know she's checking my breathing. I let her. I have so much more patience for this now that I know what happened to her mom.

"Go have a warm shower and get into some dry clothes, then come back down to the kitchen; we need to talk," Mom says, her voice tight and high.

Jenna told her.

When I come back down into the kitchen, Mom's got a mug of tea sitting at my place—Bengal Spice, my favorite. I've barely taken a sip before she leans forward, tapping the table.

"Did you call the police on Mason?"

"No, of course not." I set my mug down. "I'd never do that!" I see the cops' suspicious faces, the red-and-blue lights flashing in a sickening pattern. Feel the fear and shame again.

Mom tilts her head as she studies me with narrowed eyes. I look away. "But you know who did," she says.

"I didn't ask them to!"

Mom sighs and leans back. "It was Desi, wasn't it?"

"I didn't know what they'd done until Jenna called me." I cup my hands around my mug. "But is it such a bad thing? Mason's going to kill her one day if someone doesn't stop him." He would have already if I hadn't interrupted him. I start to wheeze.

"Take a breath, Kate. A deep breath. Good. ...Jenna said all they did was fight. That he didn't touch her."

"That's because she's too scared to admit what he's done."

"She's so angry now she won't listen to anything I say. Not that she has since she's been with Mason. You're both so strong-willed, which can be a good thing." Mom runs her hands through her hair. "But at times like this I want to shake you."

"She won't listen to me, either; she thinks I'm the one who called." I bite my lip. "But she might open up when you talk to her today," I say.

"If she talks to me at all." Mom stands abruptly. "She was pretty upset when she called." She takes the filter out of the coffee maker and dumps the grinds into the compost bin, then rinses the filter. "She accused me of taking your side, of trying to ruin her life." Mom braces herself against the counter, her shoulders hunched, head bowed, and sniffs. "Maybe I'd be better off smoothing things over."

"She didn't mean what she said," I say. "She was just upset. And if you don't confront her about Mason, nothing's going to change."

Mom takes coffee beans out of the freezer, grinds them, the sound loud, then pours them into the filter. "Maybe she didn't mean it," she says, still not looking at me. "But I think she did. She was so angry." She fills the tank with water and turns the coffee maker on, then sits back at the table with me. "I'm worried about her. Your dad and I both are."

"But not worried enough to talk to her about Mason abusing her?" I say. "Or to get Dad to?"

"I don't know, Kate," Mom says, turning her empty mug around and around. "I just don't know what the right thing to do here is. Anything I say seems to only antagonize her more." She stares off into space, looking sad, the lines on her face enunciated.

"You could try telling her first that you love her and you'll be there for her no matter what," I say.

"She knows that," Mom says sharply.

"But sometimes we need to hear those things said out loud. And with all the time you spent with me instead of her—"

"So I should've let you die?" Mom snaps, her eyes filling with tears.

The coffee maker sputters and hisses.

"No, of course not." I reach for her arm. "I'm grateful for all your help, Mom. I know I wouldn't be here without you—without all the times you've gotten my nebulizer on me, my medicine, rushed me to the hospital. I needed you. I'm sorry if I've ever made you feel like I don't. And Jenna knows that, too—but that doesn't mean she didn't feel..." I hesitate. These are things we don't usually talk about, not this overtly, but we need to. Jenna needs us to. "Unloved. Unseen."

"I love her," Mom says, her voice warbling, her hands so tight on her mug that her fingertips are white.

"I know you do. But Jenna needs to hear you say that," I say. "Maybe she'll be able to hear everything else you have to say if you do."

Mom nods, her lips pursed. "You're such an old soul sometimes."

Yeah—that's what trauma does to you. But I don't say that; I don't want to upset her more. "So you'll tell her when you see her today?"

Mom carries her mug to the counter and checks the coffee pot. "I will," she says. "But I don't think it'll make a difference."

I hope she's wrong.

Mom rinses out her mug then turns around, frowning, her mug dripping on the floor. "Listen. I saw your peak flow meter readings from this morning. If it doesn't get better tomorrow, I want you to stay home Monday."

I stiffen, about to protest, but then I sigh. "Okay."

Mom stares at me. "I'm sorry, who are you and what have you done with my daughter?"

I shrug. "You're right. Desi's been at me, too, to take better care of myself."

"I knew I liked that human!" Mom says.

"Yeah." I push my mug away.

Mom pours herself a mug of coffee, adds cream, then takes a big sip. "You have a good time with Desi?"

I shrug. "We had a fight."

Mom sits down beside me with her coffee. "You want to talk about it?"

"Not really."

Mom takes a sip of her coffee and waits.

"I don't know if we're okay," I say. "I texted them and they didn't text me back. They didn't even pick up their cell until I called maybe fifteen times. I think they broke up with me."

"What did you fight about?" Mom asks, taking another sip.

I can't tell her that I triggered an asthma attack; she'd lock me up and never let me out of the house again. "It was stupid," I say. "I was in the wrong. I need to apologize. But instead I got mad because they called the cops on Mason."

"If they matter to you then you'll apologize and talk things out, no matter how hard it feels," Mom says. "You have to clear the air in relationships, and make compromises."

"Yeah," I say. "I will."

"They were trying to protect Jenna because of what you told them, right?" Mom says, quirking her eyebrows. "You're sure that Mason is hurting her?"

"Yeah, Mom; I'm sure."

Mom takes a gulp of her coffee. "I'll see if I can get her to talk." She glances at her cell, then sets her mug down with a clatter and stands. "I'd better get going if I'm going to be there on time. You going to be okay?"

"Yeah, of course."

Mom picks her car keys up off the counter. "I'm not sure I should leave you." She studies my face. "Maybe I should call your dad, tell him to cancel his plans with Mason to stay with you."

"I'm fine," I say. "And his meeting Mason is the only way you're going to get Jenna alone. Go talk with her. Get her to open up."

Mom keeps standing there, clenching her keys.

"Really," I say. "Don't make things worse by cancelling on her. Just bring me back a cupcake. I love that bakery."

Mom brushes my hair back from my forehead. "I'd feel better if you came with me."

"Jenna wouldn't. She'd probably leave. I'll text Desi and apologize. And I promise I'll take my quick relief meds if I need to."

"All right," Mom kisses my cheek. "Phone me if your asthma acts up."

"I will," I say.

She walks down the hall to the front door. "Go easy on yourself!" she calls.

The door closes behind her, her key turning in the lock. The house feels still and empty, like it does on the days I have to stay home. Usually I don't care, but right now I feel so alone.

31

I PUSH MY MUG farther away. I can't stand to think about Desi, or Jenna or Inez, or how much I've fucked up. I want comfort food, something warm and soothing to take away the hollowness inside me.

I grab quick oats from the pantry, measure them out with water into a bowl and put it into the microwave, then grab some coconut sugar and a spoon.

The microwave beeps. I take out the bowl, sprinkle coconut sugar on top, and sit back at the table. I spoon up some oatmeal, blowing on it, then swallow the mouthful of warm comfort.

I want to call Desi right now, grovel until they give me another chance. But first I have to show them I really have changed.

I close my eyes, take a few slow breaths, and visualize Desi, Nana, and Inez, who all believe in my visions. Desi, who I love and feel loved by. I push back the tears that threaten to clog my throat. Love, only love and belief in my visions.

I breathe in and out, in and out. Love. Belief.

"Told you I'm gonna fix this," Mason says, pushing his face up close to Jenna's tear-streaked face. "Now shut up and let me get on with it."

The vision dissolves—and just like the last time I practiced, I didn't have an asthma attack, didn't even have a tight heaviness in my chest or a wheeze. It was only a fragment, but Desi and Nana are right; if I just practice more....

I breathe slowly, trying again, focusing on love, and on others' belief in me.

Inez sags in her chair, staring at a social media post, tears in her eyes.

I zoom in on the post.

Slut! You deserved it.

The vision fragments disappear. But I saw it. I saw them both. I open my eyes. I was so stupid, risking my life for no reason.

I pull out my cell and swipe to my texts. There's nothing new. But I'm the one who hurt them. I need to make the first move.

You were right and I was wrong, I text. **I was so stupid taking a risk like that. Please give me another chance. I promise I'll never trigger another attack on purpose again.**

I press send then stare at my screen, clenching my phone so hard my hand aches. My heart aches, too. Come on, Desi. I need you. I love you.

Dancing dots appear, then my cell pings.

Glad you know it. You were completely stupid risking your life like that.

I breathe out shakily. They're talking to me! That's hopeful.

I was, I absolutely was, I text. **I promise I'll never do it again. I've been practicing your nana's techniques. Got two vision fragments. I'll get better at it. Forgive me?**

Dots start and stop, start and stop. I stare at my screen, biting my lip so hard pain courses through my mouth. The dots stop moving, and there's no text.

If you give me another chance I swear I won't mess it

up, I text, my thumbs typing so fast they hurt. **I love you, Desi. I feel more alive with you. More hopeful, too. You're so compassionate and kind and book loving—the human of my dreams. Whatever it takes to earn back your trust, I'll do it. Just—please—let me.**

The dots start up again. I spoon up more oatmeal, shoving it into my mouth.

Yeah, okay. But Kate? Don't ever do that again. I need you to take care of you. Seriously. You gotta wanna live. Not have a death wish. I can't love someone who's trying not to be here.

I stare at my screen. That isn't what I was doing, but I can see how they'd take it that way. Wait—love? *Love?* I swallow tightly, my hands shaking, then type fast.

I promise I won't. I don't want to die. I'll practice getting visions your nana's way, the safe way. I want to be around—with you.

I want to be with you, too.

My heart hammers in my chest. Thank the universe they still want to be with me. **I'm so freaking glad.**

Another text pings. **And hey—I'll help you practice Nana's techniques.**

Okay. I smile goofily at my screen. **I'll do anything with you.**

Ha! I'll hold you to that... I gotta go check on Inez. Talk later?

Later!

"Yes!" I shout, pumping my fist. I laugh, breathing in deeply. Desi and I are back on. They love me, too. And everything's going to be okay. Mom's talking to Jenna, Dad's keeping Mason busy, and maybe Jenna'll finally ask for help. Desi's on Inez. And we're back together. I can't stop grinning.

I stand up and do a little twirl. Desi loves me enough that they'd break up with me so I'd see sense and not kill myself. Loves me enough to be with me again. I have another chance.

I sit back down at the table. I need to make sure Jenna does, too. I need to warn her one more time, make her see she's in danger. I shouldn't be leaving it up to Mom, who doesn't even fully believe me. With Dad keeping Mason busy, this might be my only chance.

I dial Jenna's number—and it goes straight to voicemail.

Damn it; she really did block me. The message beeps.

"Jenna, listen!" I say. "Before you delete this, just think of all the times I've been right about people—Nevaeh, Zoey, Mom's co-worker Janelle. Even your hockey buddy though I know you hated me for that. You're in danger. Mason's going to kill you. He won't do it on purpose, but he will through his beating you."

I take a shuddering breath. What will make her listen?

"I want you safe and happy. I want you to find someone who sees your strength and fierce spirit, the way you never give up when you have a goal in mind. Who'll appreciate your loyalty and stubbornness. I want all of that for you."

My voice cracks. "I want you to have the best life ever, full of laughter, love, and safety. I don't know if you've made it this far, if you're even still listening, but I love you. You're my sister. I want you alive."

I hang up and start pacing, my body full of nervous energy. I should've gone with Mom. I should be talking to Jenna in person, doing everything I can to make her hear me. I shouldn't have given up on her so easily. Her life is worth fighting for with every bit of determination I have, and every way I can think of.

I need to go tell her in person. It's harder to ignore someone when they're right in front of you. If I have to, I'll follow her home. I'll beg her to stay with us, or if she won't do that, stay at a friend's place or a shelter.

I sling my backpack over my shoulder, clenching my phone. This feels right. It's what Desi's doing with their sister—doing everything they can to keep them here.

Have I done everything I can for Inez? I think of the fragments

I got today—her reading all the hate-filled comments and messages people left. I should remind her that she's not alone, that none of it was her fault.

I call her, and it goes straight to voicemail. I leave her a message, hoping it'll help. But Desi's probably with her. I call Desi as I stride out of the kitchen.

"Kate? You okay?" Desi's voice is tight.

"Yeah. I'm on my way to talk to Jenna. But I just realized something Inez might need to hear, something from that vision fragment. Tell her that none of those bullies who left hateful comments matter. That it's the people who are with her, loving and respecting her, who do. And that she's not alone."

I choke back a laugh. Ms. Hirano's pep talk has filtered into mine. I reach for the doorknob. "Those haters aren't worth her energy. If they don't respect her, she shouldn't respect—"

The doorknob twists beneath my hand, the door wrenching open.

32

I STAGGER, THROWN OFF balance.

Mason stands in the doorway blocking out the sunlight, stinking like bad cologne and cigarettes. He puffs on a cigarette, blowing smoke into my face.

"Mason!" I cough and back up.

"Mason?" Desi says. "What do you mean?"

"Mason's—"

Mason knocks my cell out of my hand, sending it skidding across the floor. He strides after it, his leather bag bumping his hip, and stomps on my cell with his heel, the glass shattering. The screen goes black.

I scurry toward the door.

Mason slams the door shut, then whirls toward me. "Where're you going, little sister-in-law?" he asks around his cigarette.

My skin prickles. "You're supposed to be with my dad."

"Yeah. I saw through that, bitch. Tag-teaming us so your mom can drip poison in Jenna's ear, get her to leave me." He clenches his hands.

I back up a step.

Mason walks closer, puffing harder on his cigarette, blowing smoke at me.

I take another step backward, coughing. "Desi knows you're

here."

"So? I'm just having a nice, friendly talk with my sister-in-law who's been hallucinating."

I turn and run toward the backyard.

Mason yanks me back. "I didn't say you could go." He blows more smoke into my face.

I gasp for air and wrench at his grip, trying to get away. His fingers dig deep into my arm, pressing on bone. My lungs clench against the smoke and I cough-wheeze. I've got to get outside. I punch his gut, but he just swats my fist away.

My heart's beating so loudly it sounds like thunder. I yank at his grip desperately. "Let go of me!"

He pulls me back against his chest, his arm around my neck. "Not on your life."

I fumble for my inhaler, my vision blurring.

Mason's arm tightens around Jenna as she leans against him. "Kate sure has a lot of asthma attacks."

"She always has, ever since she was a baby." Jenna rests her hand on Mason's chest. "But why're we talking about her? You're always saying she takes up too much of my headspace. And I'm just as mad at her as you are."

"I don't think you can be," Mason says, pulling his arm away. "I don't take kindly to people betraying us. But she's your sister, so I wanna know her better. What sets her asthma off?"

Jenna rolls her eyes. "Everything."

Mason laughs, then tips his beer bottle back, taking a swallow. "No, seriously."

"Since when do you care?" Jenna says.

Mason sets his beer down and squeezes the back of her neck, then moves to the front of her throat, smoothing her skin, stroking it. "I care about you, so this matters to me. Now tell me what sets her off."

Jenna swallows. "Anything that irritates her lungs. Cigarettes are really bad. And pollen. Air pollution. Aerosol sprays. Strong cleaners. Perfume and cologne. That's why Mom tells you not to smoke even outside the house. Kate is really sensitive."

Mason lets Jenna go and takes another sip of his beer. "If she has a really bad attack, can she die?"

"Yeah." Jenna shivers. "She almost did a few times. It was really scary."

God. I shudder. That's why Mason showed up here smoking and stinking of cologne. He's trying to kill me.

My arm's hurting, my body's moving, bumping over the floor, but I'm not walking. I blink hard to clear my vision. Mason's dragging me across the room. I bite his arm.

"Bitch!" He slaps my face so hard my teeth rattle and my glasses get knocked askew, then drags me into the kitchen.

I gasp harder, my vision blurring again.

"What set off her worst attacks?" Mason asks.

Jenna pushes him away. "You're starting to sound like my parents. All they ever talk about is Kate."

Mason grips Jenna's wrist so tight she winces. "I'm nothing like them. I'm the only one who loves you this much, remember?"

"I know," Jenna says. "You love me the most."

Mason takes another swallow of his beer. "That's right."

Jenna kisses him. "I'm late for my shift at the bakery. You'd better go, too, or you'll be late."

Mason scowls at her. "I'll go when I'm good and ready."

Mason presses his face close to mine, exhaling more smoke. "You're gonna pay for hurting Jenna. For hurting us."

"I didn't call the police on you," I say, coughing and wheezing as I struggle to jerk out of his grip. I punch at him, but he hangs on harder, pain blooming through me.

"Yeah. Like I believe that." Mason shoves me down into a kitchen chair, whipping out a roll of silver duct tape from his bag.

I jump up, coughing, my legs wobbling, and yank my inhaler from my pocket. He punches my chest so hard I can't hear or see anything for a moment, my breath gone, wheeze-gasping. He slaps my face, knocking my glasses off. They clatter against the floor. Everything blurs harder.

"Stupid queer." He punches my arm. I drop my inhaler, my fingers numb.

"Stay put!" he yells, ramming me back down. He tapes me to the chair, my chest heaving. "You've hurt too many people. And not just Jenna and me. You hurt everyone you try to help. I know 'cause Jenna told me all about it." He grins at me around his cigarette. "That girl who was kidnapped, your mom's coworker, you scared them before anything even happened to them. You made them suffer."

I see their scared, upset faces. He's right.

No—I tried to help them. They weren't ready to believe it, but I tried—and trying and failing is better than never trying at all. I cared enough to speak the truth even when people thought I was lying. I was brave, even when I thought I wasn't.

I didn't run away from my gift like Desi's mom, or at least I came back to it. And that might be enough to save Jenna and Inez. I hope it is.

"So I'm gonna make you suffer," Mason says, ripping off the end of the duct tape. "And then I'm gonna stop you from hurting anyone ever again." He stomps his foot, the crunch loud. My glasses.

My lips wobble. I shake my head to jumpstart my brain. "You can't kill me like this," I say, my voice hoarse and cracked. "No one'll believe this was an accident."

Mason jams the cigarette he was smoking into my unfinished oatmeal so it stands like a stick of incense, spewing smoke. Then he takes a pack of cigarettes out of his shirt pocket, shakes one out and lights it. He jams it in beside the first one. "That's the trouble with you educated chicks; you think you're smarter than the rest of us. All I gotta do is cut you loose when I'm done, air the place out, and no one'll know the difference. Or maybe I saw you with a friend who was smoking—that girl you like. Then it'll all be on her."

"No!" I cough harder, my legs trembling, knees bouncing up and down. Mason lights another cigarette, then another, stuffing them upright into the oatmeal. He really is going to kill me. The room grows even hazier, dots jittering before my eyes.

Another vision's coming. If drawing on love and belief can help me have visions without having an asthma attack, maybe it can help lessen the severity while I'm having one.

I think of Desi, my mom, how much I love them, how they love me, and pull it to me. I know my visions are real, and I know they're meant to help others. They did help Zoey in the end. And they would've helped me protect more people if others had believed me.

I wheeze, my lungs spasming. My visions even tried to help me, telling me about Mason. Maybe they can help me again, give me something I can use about him. I shudder-gasp. I can't focus on Mason with love, but I can focus on myself. I open myself up to the vision, the room blurring even harder.

Mason sits in a small wood shack drinking beer, a rifle in his lap, hand gun on the table next to dozens of empty beer bottles.

Wheels crunch on gravel, then two police cars pull up. Mason grabs his rifle, runs to the window, and shoots.

"Shots fired!" The officers run behind their cars, take aim, and shoot.

Mason staggers back, blood blooming on his shoulder. Another bullet hits his arm, and he falls to the floor, cursing, blood still blooming.

Thank you, I tell my visions silently. They gave me what I needed. They've been helping me all along.

I cough-wheeze, blinking, wishing I could see the room more

clearly. "If you kill me," I say, my voice raspy and hoarse, "You'll die, too. I just saw your death." Well, technically I saw him get shot, but I hope it'll be enough to scare him into letting me go.

Mason narrows his eyes at me. "Bullshit." He lights another cigarette.

"I saw the police shoot you," I say, wheezing harder.

Mason stuffs the lit cigarette into the oatmeal with the others. "I'd kill them first," he says, but his hand trembles.

"You don't have the chance," I say, wheeze-coughing. "There are too many of them."

"Bullshit!" Mason yells. He lights another cigarette. "I call bullshit. You're a liar, just like your sister, hiding her pregnancy from me." He jams the cigarette into the oatmeal.

I reach for the blurry shape of my inhaler with my foot, knocking it toward me. It's so close, but I can't pick it up. I wheeze-cough harder. "It's true."

What can I say to convince him? Some details only he would know. "You were sitting at a rickety old wood table," I cough-gasp, "In a wood shack, empties around you, a rifle in your lap."

"A shack?" Mason's lips curl up, exposing his teeth. "Jenna told you about that."

I pull the vision to me, focusing on the walls. "There's a dart board with my photo on it."

Mason freezes, staring at me. "You're ungodly."

Interesting word choice. I cough. "Thou shalt not kill." Cough. "You're the ungodly one."

His hands tremble, but he keeps lighting cigarettes.

At least the HEPA air filter is working. The filter hums louder, a beep sounding. Maybe it'll keep me alive.

Mason follows my gaze, strides over, and yanks out the plug.

I strain against the duct tape. I'm not ready to die. I want to make sure Jenna and Inez will live. I want to kiss Desi again, go on real dates, maybe live with them someday. I want to mend my relationship with Jenna. And build one with my mom.

I shudder and heave against the tape, trying to loosen it. I want Mom and Dad to believe my visions and know that I can help others. I want to go to Pride with Desi, walk in protests, attend queer art shows, read all the books that fill me with queer joy or help me feel less alone. I want to find more friends and community, go to college, maybe even have kids someday. I want to *live*. I cough harder, my lungs clenching and spasming against the smoke.

Pulling love to me helped before.

I envision Desi's face, then Mom's and Dad's, and finally Jenna's. I think of how much I love and need them. I see their smiles, the love in their eyes, and their love fills me, strengthening me. My lungs expand, even as my vision blurs more.

Jenna punches a number into her cell as she walks toward the bakery. "Come on, Kate, pick up!" She hails a taxi and jumps in. "Please let me be wrong," she keeps saying on the ride over.

Jenna bursts through our front door and runs into the kitchen to find me taped to the chair, head hanging, chest still, the cigarettes burned down to the butts in the oatmeal. Mason's opening the kitchen windows.

Jenna shakes me, my head lolling, my fingertips and lips blue.

"What did you do?" she screams at Mason. "You murderer!"

Mason relights one of the cigarettes that went out. Then he takes an aerosol can out of his bag, shakes it, and sprays it around the room, the mist like heavy fog. "Having a little trouble breathing?" he says with a grin.

"Don't!" I cough. My chest is so heavy and tight I can barely suck in the smoky, chemical-laden air.

"Already doing it." Mason keeps spraying, the hissing sound filling my ears.

I cough-choke so hard I can't breathe in. The puke-green kitchen walls undulate blurrily in front of me. "Jenna will never—" cough "—forgive you. She's coming—" Cough. *"Now."*

Mason hesitates, his finger loosening on the aerosol button, his arm shaking. "Freak," he whispers.

If I can just get loose from the tape and grab my inhaler... I yank harder, jerking my whole body again and again, reaching for it.

The chair topples over, the tile coming up fast. Pain bursts through my shoulder, my head, little bits of broken plastic and glass cutting into my skin.

Mason laughs, braying like a donkey. "Now you've done it. You can just stay there."

What else can I say to make him stop?

I try to breathe shallowly. Maybe the truth. It's already shaking him. "I told Jenna about you—" Cough. "Because I saw you kill her." I cough harder.

Mason empties the aerosol can in the air, then takes another out. "Now I know you're lying. I'd never kill her; I love her!"

"You didn't mean to—" Cough. "But you did. That's why Desi and I—" Cough "Came that day to your place." I cough so hard it feels like my lungs are forcing themselves up through my throat. "We stopped you killing her." Cough. "You were hitting her—" Cough. The pain in my chest is like fire. "Smashing her head against the wall." His face fades in and out. "You cried. Didn't mean to."

Mason stares at me, his face pale, mouth open.

"And now—" Cough. "Without me to stop you," Cough. "You will kill her." Cough. Even if this doesn't save me, maybe it'll save Jenna.

My lungs are shrivelling up. I can't get enough air. Blackness edges into my vision. I cough so hard, I choke.

"And this—" Cough. "Will kill her love for you."

Mason slaps the aerosol can down. "It won't," he says hoarsely.

"It will—" Cough "I saw it."

Mason hesitates again.

My lips and fingers are numb. I'm so dizzy I don't even know if I'm still attached to the chair, but I must be; I can't get up. I hack harder. I'm going to die. Jenna will never forgive herself. Mom and Dad will be shattered. Desi will be hurt. "She'll hate you."

"No," Mason says, his voice cracking.

"Your killing me makes her leave you."

"No!" Mason shouts. He yanks out a pocket knife, jerking it open, and charges towards me.

I stiffen, coughing. I'm going to die sooner than I thought.

33

MASON KNEELS IN FRONT of me and slices open the duct tape.

I fall onto my stomach. My chest hurts like a bus is lying on top of it. The blue tile floor is covered in tiny droplets of aerosol spray like rain. My head lolls to the side. I gasp, trying to breathe, my heart pumping so hard it feels like it might burst.

"Mason!" Jenna screeches. Footsteps pound.

Desi's face appears in front of mine. I must be hallucinating. They grab my inhaler, prime it, and whisper in my ear. "Breathe."

I try to, but I can barely pull in air, just a trickle. I suck in as much as I can.

Jenna's voice rises and falls; I strain to bring her words into focus.

"You murderer!" Jenna screams, her fists clenched, body shaking.

"I did it to protect you!" Mason shouts. "To protect *us*!"

Don't let me die. I raise my head. "Nebulizer," I croak. It's not loud, but it's enough. I'm coughing again, struggling for air, the pain in my lungs like my chest has been cut open.

"Jenna, where's her nebulizer?" Desi shouts.

Desi came. They both did. I hope I live to thank them. Desi yanks out their cell and taps 911. "I need an ambulance," they whisper.

"Over here!" Jenna calls, grabbing my nebulizer.

I cough-gasp, weaker now, the pain like an iron bar through each lung.

"What's she doing here?" Mason yells.

"They found the backup door key," Jenna says, rushing towards us with my nebulizer. "And lucky they did or you'd be facing murder charges. You might still."

"What're you doing?" Mason yells, yanking Jenna around so hard her head jerks back. "She'll tell them what I did. I'll go to jail."

"If you kill her, I'll send you to jail myself!" Jenna shrieks, punching his chest. She starts towards us.

"Jenna, no!" Mason yells. "I'll stop. I promise. We'll leave town, just you and me."

Jenna ignores him and runs over, slapping the mask onto my face, pouring medicine in, and starting it up. "Help her sit up."

Desi sits me up, leaning me against them on the floor. "Breathe, mi cielo." They put the phone back to their ear. "Yes, I'm still here."

I gasp for air, every movement ripping pain through my chest, my throat, my head.

Mason stalks towards us. "Get out! This is a family matter." He lunges for their phone.

"Stop it, just stop it!" Jenna cries, rising and pounding his chest. "If you love me, stop it."

Desi rattles off our address to the dispatcher. Their face goes in and out of focus.

Mason looms over me, clenching and unclenching his fists. "You do this, you're turning your back on us, babe. You're turning your back on me."

"You don't know what you're saying," Jenna says, tears streaming down her face.

"The hell I do. She was getting in the way of you and me. She was fucking us up."

"No, what you did is fucked up." Jenna runs to open a window. The room spins around me. "I'll never be able to forgive you."

When I open my eyes again, I'm still leaning against Desi's chest. They're telling me over and over to breathe, to stay, that they need me, their tears falling onto me.

Jenna pours more medicine into my nebulizer. "Breathe, honey."

"Mason ran," Desi says.

I try to suck in the medicine but I can't get enough air.

Sirens shriek close by.

I'm so weak, my head dizzy.

"Kate, hang on! Breathe!" Desi says, tears in their voice. "The ambulance is here. Just hang on a little longer."

I want to tell them I'm trying, but I can't speak.

Sound and vision fade in and out.

Inez stares at the bottles of medication on her desk, her shoulders slumped. She flicks through her cell, pausing at comment after comment full of hate. She stops on a comment from her ex: You deserved it. *Slowly, she opens all the bottles of pills on her desk.*

It wasn't just anonymous haters. And all that hate must make her feel so hopeless, especially from someone she thought loved her. I've got to tell Desi.

I shake my head, gasping. Tubes are stuffed up my nose, oxygen flooding into me. "Easy, hon. Just keep breathing," a woman in a black uniform says. A siren wails, a machine beeping as the ambulance sways.

Inez's cell rings and rings. She hesitates, pills in her hand, but finally answers it. "What?"

"Inez—Mason tried to kill Kate!"

Inez's back straightens, her eyes stretching wide. "What?"

"I'm on my way to the hospital," Desi says, their voice breaking. "She might not make it. I—I need her to live, Inez. I need you both to."

Inez shivers, hugging herself with one arm. "I know you do," she says softly. "Tell Kate to hang in there, and I will, too. She's stronger than that asshole. And I'm stronger than my ex and my rapists. You tell her that."

"I will," Desi cries, their voice hoarse. "But Inez, I don't think I can handle this alone."

"You don't have to," Inez says, standing shakily. "I'm coming. I'll meet you there." She grabs her keys and purse, hesitating at her desk, looking at the pill bottles.

"Really?" Desi asks, gasping. "Are you sure?"

"I'm sure," Inez says. "See you soon. Remind Kate to pull love to her."

She hangs up, gathers her pill bottles and strides to the bathroom, then flushes the pills down the toilet.

At least Inez will be okay. I cough and cough, feeling like I'm drowning. Panic is like a bird's talons ripping through my chest. I have to keep calm and feel the love, like Inez said. I visualize Desi, Jenna, Mom and Dad, their arms holding me tight. For a second, I almost feel like I can breathe.

The paramedics wheel my stretcher into the hospital, lights passing overhead. Shouts sound out, and a nurse runs up. My chest heaves. I can't stop coughing.

Inez hesitates at her door. "If you can see this, Kate, know that I'm gonna talk on social media, tell the truth about what my ex and rapists did—as long as you hang in there. Okay? You survive, and I'll work on speaking out. On healing. Because my Desi needs you. And I do, too. I need to know we can survive these toxic men."

She runs out to the kitchen, calling for Nana.

The fight and determination in her words and voice makes me glad.

A doctor is in my face, talking to me loudly. I'm a fish out of water, gasping and unable to breathe.

Mason drives down the highway, looking over his shoulder. He turns onto a dirt road and pulls up at a shack. He barricades the door from inside, then takes a shotgun off the wall, and beer from the fridge. He sits at a rickety wood table, pointing the gun at the door, turns the TV to the news, and opens his first bottle of beer.

I'm dying. I can feel it. My lungs are shutting down. I focus on Desi, on their love for me, on Mom and Dad and Jenna, and Inez and Nana, too. "Help me," I tell them. For a breath, then another, I breathe easier. But it's too hard and I'm too tired. I close my eyes.

When I open my eyes again, I'm lying in a hospital bed in a small white room. Everything's fuzzy—my glasses still broken and gone. There's a tube down my throat, a mask on my face, and a ventilator pumping oxygen in and out of my lungs. A machine beeps annoyingly. My chest aches fiercely, and I'm so exhausted I want to cry, but I'm alive. I try to swallow and gag on the plastic tube.

They've intubated me. That isn't a good sign. I weakly turn my head. Jenna's sitting in a chair next to my bed. She leaps up and grabs my hand. Her nose and eyelids are red and swollen.

"I'm sorry, Kate," she whispers. "I didn't know he'd try to hurt you; I swear I didn't. I didn't even know he'd taken my key."

I make tapping motions with my thumbs, miming texting.

"Oh!" Jenna digs around in a pile of clothes heaped on the chair, grabs my cell and hands it to me.

I know you didn't know. It's not your fault, I text, peering at the screen. **Did you tell Mom and Dad? They should change the locks. Where are they?**

Jenna's cell pings. She fumbles in her purse and pulls it out, reading it. "Yeah, I did. They're talking to the cops. Want me to get them?"

I shake my head.

Jenna looks down. "When Mason asked me about your asthma, at first I thought he was just being nice to me. Trying to understand why..." Her cheeks darken.

Why you resented me? I text. **Because I got all the attention.**

Jenna's shoulders slump as she reads what I wrote. "Yeah. It's stupid. I know you get really sick. That you could die. I know you needed Mom—"

But you needed her too, I text fast. **I would've been jealous too.**

"Why're you being so nice to me?" Jenna cries, clenching her cell.

You're my big sis. I love you.

"I love you, too," Jenna says, tears in her eyes. "I don't know how I'll ever make this right—"

Not your fault, I text again.

Jenna shakes her head. "I knew he was the jealous type. Obsessive. Controlling..." Her voice trails off. "I'm going to leave him," she says uncertainly.

Good, I text. I swipe open a note app, type in more. **You're strong, and you're smart to leave him. He was hurting you.** I hold my cell up for her to see.

Jenna frowns, then leans forward to read my screen. "Yeah. He was."

You need to ditch your phone, I type. **He was spying on you with it.** I hold up my cell again for her to read.

Jenna gasps. "That's how he knew what we'd talked about."

Yes. I just saw it today. Promise to get a new one? Trade yours in for a different one? Or hire someone to remove the spyware. Load on extra protection.

"Yes! Right away."

A nurse passes by in the hall, her shoes squeaking. My energy is starting to ebb. I grit my teeth, try to push through the exhaustion. I have to ask Jenna. But still, I hesitate. **Are the police looking for**

him? I type in the notes app.

Jenna leans over to look at my screen. "Yes."

I hesitate again. **Do you want to tell them where he is?**

Jenna wrinkles her nose. "But I don't know."

I wait for her to put it together. I don't want to push her away again.

Jenna stares at me, her eyes growing wider. "Oh. *You* know?"

I nod.

"Because of your visions?"

I nod again.

"Mason said you knew I was coming. That you'd seen what I'd say to him." Jenna twirls the end of her hair, the way she used to do when she was anxious. "Okay. Tell me. I'll tell the police. It's the least I can do."

You sure? I write.

Jenna squares her shoulders. "Yes. It'll be a very small way I can help put this right."

You don't have anything to put right. He's at a hunting shack in woods. His family's? I hold up my cell for her.

"Yeah, I know where that is. I'll tell the police," Jenna says soberly.

He has a shotgun and a handgun, and he's very drunk. He's going to shoot at them, and they'll shoot back. I told him that. Tell the cops to be careful, I type.

"That sounds like Mason," Jenna says. She looks down at the polished linoleum floor. "When Desi and I found you, I thought you were dead. You were limp, lying on the floor. I—" Jenna bursts into tears.

I reach for her hand and squeeze it, the IV tugging at my skin. Jenna keeps crying.

"That was the worst moment of my life." Jenna dries her cheek with her wrist. "I'm sorry I was so mean to you when you were trying to help me. I was scared of Mason when he hurt me—he can be a mean son-of-a-bitch—but afterwards he'd always treat me like I was the most special person on earth. He'd shower me with gifts, tell me he loved me, that he needed me, that he couldn't live without me. And he'd tell me it'd never happen again. I wanted to believe him so badly."

That must've been really hard, I type, holding up my cell.

"Yeah," Jenna says, tears filling her eyes again. "It was. But I shouldn't have blamed you, even if he did. I shouldn't have been mean."

It's okay, I text. **Is Desi here?**

Jenna's cell pings. She half laughs, half cries. "Yes. They're so worried about you—just as much as we all are. Maybe more."

My heart pounds faster. **Where are they?**

"In the waiting room. They wanted to see you, but the doctors only let family in when...when someone's as sick as you were."

I can't believe I triggered my asthma on purpose. I wanted Jenna to escape, and Inez to stay alive. But my life isn't something I should take a chance with. Especially when there were other ways to help. I hope Desi really has forgiven me.

I want to see them as soon as I can, I text.

Jenna smirks, reading her cell. "I know. I'll tell them."

And tell them I'm okay? Thank them for coming? And...tell them I'm sorry I didn't listen to them.

"You really like them, don't you?" Jenna says, tilting her head as she looks at me.

I nod.

"Did they actually try to talk some sense into you, get you to be more proactive about your health?" Jenna says, lightly shoving my arm.

I roll my eyes, then nod again.

"Good for them," Jenna says, laughing. "I like them."

I roll my eyes again. If I could smile around the tube, I would.

Still mad at me? I text.

"For what, for god's sake?" Jenna asks.

For pushing you about Mason, I type into my note app, then hold up my cell.

Jenna's cheeks flush. "I needed to be pushed. You were right. Look what he did to you!" She rubs her arms.

And to you, I write in the note app. **And he could've hurt the baby.**

Jenna looks at my screen for a long time. "Yes," she says finally. She turns her gaze on me and slowly lifts up her shirt. Her ribs and stomach are covered in deep purple, brown, and yellow bruises. I shudder and she yanks her shirt back down.

God! Jenna. You need to get a dr to check you, I type.

"I will. I promise. I feel like I can think again, without Mason around." She rests her hand on her stomach. "I'll take care of the little one."

So you're going to keep the baby?

She nods, her eyes tearing up. "It's not their fault their daddy is a jerk. It'll be hard, but I've got Dad and Mom for support. And you, right?"

Absolutely. But are you sure that's what you want?

Jenna rubs her eyes, the skin dark beneath them. "No. I'm not sure at all. But I've still got time to decide."

Whatever you decide, I'll support you, I type. **It's your body. Your life that it'll affect.**

Jenna smiles a watery smile. "Thank you." She looks at me and moistens her lips. "You really can see things, can't you? The future, I mean?"

Yes.

"And did you—" She hesitates. "Did you see anything about this?"

No. Just what I told you. And unless it would help prevent trauma, I'm not sure I'd tell her if I did. She has to decide what's best for her about something as important as this. **I used to only see things when I got an asthma attack. Now I can sometimes if**

I focus. But I can't control what I see.

"Wow," Jenna says, shaking her head. "And damn. That must be hard." She wraps her arms around herself. "I'm sorry I never believed you—even though you were right every time. Even though I knew you were right about Mason. I just—" She looks up at the ceiling, blinking back tears.

It's all right, I text.

She glances at her cell. "No, it's not. You've been trying to help people, to stop tragedies, and I just assumed you were trying to get more attention. All the attention. I was...projecting."

I can't believe she's actually empathizing with me. I wish I could hug her. **Thank you,** I text. **And I'm sorry my being sick took attention away from you.**

"God, Kate," Jenna says, tears in her voice. She leans down and hugs me.

I hug her back. I can't remember the last time she hugged me first and it felt like she wanted to. Like she meant it. Tears burn my eyes, and a few escape.

Jenna pulls back. "What's wrong?"

I've got my sister back.

"Yeah, you do," Jenna says. "Just stop scaring me by almost dying, okay? And get better fast." She shoulders her purse. "I'll let Dad and Mom know you're awake. And then I'll tell the police where Mason is." She leans over and kisses my cheek. "It could've been me Mason tried to kill. It almost was." Jenna chokes up.

She has no idea how close she came to actually being killed.

"Thank you for being such a great sister," she says, then hurries out of the room before I can tell her that she's a great sister, too. Or she's becoming one.

34

I WAKE TO THE rumble of a trolley going by. The tube is still in my throat, the ventilator breathing for me with a loud, whooshing sound. Mom and Dad are both sitting beside my bed, their skin washed out in the fluorescent light. I can see them more clearly. How? I struggle to sit up more.

Mom jumps up and comes to my side. "You're going to be okay, honey," she says tearfully, stroking my head. "You're going to be just fine."

I think she needs that reassurance more than I do. I touch my face. I'm wearing glasses.

"We brought your old glasses," Mom says. "Jenna told us."

Dad comes over on my other side and squeezes my shoulder. "You sure gave us a scare."

I look for my cell. Mom grabs it from the bed table and hands it to me. I open a new document in my notes app. Mason tried to kill me, I type. I hold it up for them to see.

Mom takes my cell, staring at the screen, then hands it to Dad. "We know, honey," she says in a choked voice. "Jenna told us. But it's all over now. The police are out looking for him, and he's never going to hurt you again."

"I'll kill him first," Dad says, gripping my shoulder so hard it hurts. He hands me back my cell.

I hate how weak I was, I type. **He didn't have to do much. Light a few cigarettes, wear some bad cologne, spray some air freshener...**

Mom reaches for my cell, frowning as she reads. "You are *not* weak," she says firmly. "You have asthma. We can't change that. Yes, your triggers make you vulnerable. But you tried to get away. You knew to use your inhaler. You did all the right things. And you survived."

"And you're the only one who saw Mason for who he really was," Dad says. "You had the courage to speak up when no one else believed you. I'm proud of you, Katie. We both are."

I "saw" what he did in my visions, I type.

Dad reads my cell, then hands it to Mom.

Mom nods. "Jenna told us everything you said was true; she just didn't want to admit it." Mom takes a deep breath. "I'm sorry we didn't believe you. It's a lot to wrap our heads around—that you really can see the future. It just sounds so unbelievable, so sci-fi-ish." She hands me back my cell.

But you believe me now? I type.

"Yes," Mom says. She hands my cell to Dad. "This whole thing with Jenna convinced me. And..." She breaks off, tears in her eyes. "I remember that girl with asthma you said would die that day if they didn't intervene. You were right. And Janelle, my co-worker, who you knew was going to get hit by a drunk driver. And Zoe—that girl. I thought you just had a good intuition and a very active imagination. But there've been too many times that you were right."

"We can only say we're sorry, and that we'll believe you from here on out," Dad says. "And anyone who doesn't can go to hell. But...it's probably not a good thing to mention to the doctors, Katie. We don't want them trying to figure out what's wrong with you just because they don't believe it." He hands me back my cell.

I know, I type. **I only tell people when I have to.**

"You're smart," Dad says, squeezing my hand. "You always have been."

After all these years of desperately wanting Mom and Dad to believe me, it feels surreal that they suddenly do. Maybe it's their reaction to the crisis—to me almost dying, to Jenna being beaten, to Mason on the run. I guess I'll find out whether they still believe me next time I have a vision. Although maybe there's something I can do to help that along.

Desi's nana has psychic gifts, too. She's a medium. Maybe you can talk to her sometime? I type.

Dad reads it first, then passes my cell silently to Mom. Mom strokes my cheek. "Sure, honey. We'll talk to her."

Dad clears his throat. "Why don't we invite them all over for dinner when you're doing better?"

They're trying. They really are. Okay, I write.

I shift restlessly. I hate this tube in my mouth. Hate a machine breathing for me. I want to go home. Want to feel normal again.

Jenna said Desi was here, I write. **Did she tell them I'm okay? Can they visit yet?**

"When your tube is out and you're breathing on your own," Mom says firmly. "They can visit then."

I frown at her around the tube, but I know there's no changing her mind. She's fiercely overprotective. But then, she's had to be. Still, I can try. **Just for a few minutes?**

"Kate Robbins, you almost died. You will lie there and rest and get better," Mom says. "When the tube is out is soon enough."

I try to sigh and end up coughing, which is extra painful with the breathing tube in.

Mom rushes forward, pushing me upright to make breathing easier until the coughing fit stops. I nod weakly at her, tears leaking from my eyes, and sink back into my pillow.

"You see? You're not ready yet," Mom says. "And when you're better, the police will want to interview you."

"I think she gets that," Dad says.

Could you bring my backpack from home? I type.

"Yes, of course honey," Mom says.

Dad looks at me. "We should let you rest."

I shake my head, then type Wait! on my cell. They wait.

Are you okay with all the police? I type.

"Why wouldn't we be?" Mom asks, then stops herself. "Oh, honey—are you talking about that girl...about Zoey—?" Her voice breaks off. "That wasn't your fault. And you were right after all."

But I remember the hours and hours the officers spent interrogating me and each of my parents. The suspicion and anger that resonated off the officers, and the haunted look my parents wore for months. The news stories about Zoey being abducted—which I'd predicted. The way the cops treated us as if we were the ones who'd snatched her, especially Dad, all because I'd seen pieces of it before it happened. The way even our neighbors shunned us, their eyes slitted and cold.

You really don't blame me? I write.

"Honey, no! And if we'd understood sooner and believed you, maybe it would've turned out different."

I look at Dad, wondering if he feels the same way. How can he?

He nods. "Everything your mother said, sweetheart." He smooths back my hair. "We can talk later. Why don't you rest?"

I close my eyes and let sleep take me.

My throat feels raw, but at least I can swallow and talk now that the tube is out. It's a relief to breathe on my own. Though now I can smell that mixture of disinfectant and canned air that seems to pervade every hospital. I sigh. My chest hurts deep inside, but at least I'm not coughing any more. And I have my own pajamas, instead of that awful thin hospital gown that opens at the back and always makes me feel exposed.

Mom looks at me from her seat beside me. "Everything okay?"

"Yeah," I say hoarsely. I pick my book back up, a queer YA rom-com Mom got me—*Going Bicoastal*. I push my old glasses up onto the top of my head; it's easier to read without them.

Dad's back at work, Jenna's talking to a counselor, and I'm just waiting to go home. Out the window, the sky looks clear and blue and perfect.

Dad strides in, smiling broadly, carrying a bulging bubble-wrap envelope. "Got something for you, kiddo."

"What?"

"Open it and see," Dad says, shoving the package at me.

I can't believe he left work to bring me mail. I push my old glasses back down over my nose, and rip the package open. It's a rainbow eyeglasses case. I suck in my breath, opening the case with stiff fingers. Glasses with rainbow frames.

My eyes burn. I force my lips to stop trembling.

"Just like the ones you had," Dad says gruffly. "Go one, put them on, make sure they're right."

I take off my old glasses, put on my new ones. Dad's and Mom's faces come into sharper focus. "You got these for me?" I say, staring at him.

"I know they were important to you," Dad says. He runs his hand through his hair. "And I know I haven't always been, you know, the most supportive. But I'm trying."

He sure is. "Thank you," I say hoarsely, reaching for his firm hand and squeezing it.

Mom watches us tearily, dabbing at her eyes beneath her glasses.

There's a rap on the doorframe, and then Desi and Inez walk in, Inez hanging on tightly to Desi's arm. Gone are Inez's sweat pants and greasy hair; she's wearing jeans and a T-shirt, her hair washed and combed. And Desi's wearing a bright fuchsia button-down shirt with a Monarch butterfly tie, tight jeans, and purple docs, their backpack slung over one shoulder. They look so good I want to kiss them.

"Hey!" I say hoarsely. "I'm so glad you came!" I let my gaze linger on Desi for only a moment then smile at Inez, trying to reassure her. I know it took courage for her to leave the apartment for only the second time since she was raped.

"Hi Kate, hi Mrs. and Mr. Robbins," Desi says.

"Hi," Inez says uncertainly, her hands clenched together.

Mom smooths her dress and stands. "We'll give you three some alone time. All right, sweetie?" Mom pats my knee.

"Thanks," I say.

"Wait, what?" Dad says. "I just got here."

Mom grabs his arm and drags him out the door.

Inez walks to the edge of my bed and tentatively touches my shoulder. "How're you feeling?"

"Better. I can go home soon," I say hoarsely.

"Are you really going to be okay?" Inez says. "Desi says you almost died."

"Yeah. I'm hanging in. Glad to see you are, too." I study her. Her eyes look brighter, her face less troubled than the last time I saw her—both in person and in my visions. There's still pain behind her eyes, but it doesn't look as intense. "I hope you're not thinking about a way out anymore," I say.

Inez shakes her head. "No; you were right. It'd hurt Desi and my nana too much. And I think I want to live now—the way you do. I want to change things for the better. I can't do that if I'm dead."

"Exactly," I say and cough.

Desi leaps forward. "You need your inhaler? Oxygen?"

I laugh, even though it hurts to. "I'm okay, Desi. My throat's just a little raw. I'll survive."

"Okay." Desi laughs shakily. "You scared the shit out of me, you know."

"I know. I'm sorry."

Inez cracks her knuckles. "I want you to know I'm okay now. Well, I *will* be okay. I'm getting better." Inez swallows hard. "Desi told me what you did. You don't have to risk your life any more to see my future. I'll be okay."

"You promise?" I look at her steadily, knowing that if she promises she'll keep moving toward life. Toward healing.

"Yeah, I promise," Inez says, nodding curtly.

"I'm glad," I say. "Did you tell the others you got rid of your pills?"

Inez laughs. "I shouldn't be surprised; you seem to see everything! Yeah, I told them. I did it as soon as I heard you were in trouble."

"Good." I bite back more questions. Maybe she decided not to talk about her abuse. I don't want her to feel worse.

"I'm going to make some videos about what my rapists and ex did to me," Inez says. "And post them on social media. I made a deal with you, or god, if you survived. I'll bet you saw that, too."

"I did," I say, smiling awkwardly. "But listen—only do if it truly feels right to you. I won't hold you to it. The only thing I'll hold you to is that you stay."

Inez raises her chin. "No; I want to. It's the right thing, to speak out—and this is the way I can do it. The cops, the justice system—I don't trust that that wouldn't crush me. But this way? This will help others, let them know they're not alone. And I think it might help me, too."

"I'm glad. I hope it helps you feel like you're taking back your power." I cough. "Because it's hella brave. And you're right—it's helping others. And yourself. And if it gets to be too much, you can take the videos down."

Inez raises her chin even higher. "I won't."

"I'm so proud of you," Desi cries, hugging her tight.

"Thanks." Inez's face flushes darker. "I'll just go get something from the vending machine. Come find me when you're done, Desi."

Desi watches her leave, then turns to me. "Thank you for saving her."

"You helped, too. It wasn't all me. And Inez had to want to be here. She's the one who really saved herself."

"But she needed our help." Desi shakes their head. "I didn't even know she was planning to kill herself until you told me. If it hadn't been for you—" They suck in their breath sharply. "I don't even want to think about it." Desi unslings their backpack and pulls out a wrapped package, thrusting it at me. "This is for you."

I rip open the wrapping paper. Two books: *Felix Ever After* and *Can't Take that Away*.

"I know you love books," they say. "I thought, while you're recovering, you might want to read a few with nonbinary characters. I mean, if you want to." They shift their feet.

"That's perfect! I do want to," I say hoarsely and grin at them. "Thank you; that was so thoughtful. I actually got you one, too—though you might've read it already. And one thing I made. Sorry I didn't have time to wrap them."

Desi snorts. "No worries."

"They're in my backpack," I say, pointing to the chair where my mom was sitting.

Desi grabs my backpack and pulls out the book first. "I love *Sir Callie* so much!" they say. "I've wanted my own copy for a while now."

"Good," I say. "And there's one more thing—"

Desi's already reaching back into my knapsack. They pull out the paper-bag book I made—all the things I like about them.

They flip through the pages, their eyes shimmering with tears. "This means so much. I love what you said. Thank you." They walk back over to my side, pressing their fist to their lips. "I'm sorry I didn't get to your place sooner. I should've protected you."

"Are you kidding? You got there just in time." I grab their hand. "I'm so grateful you figured out I was in danger. But how'd you get in? Mason had Jenna's key."

"Los espiritus, the spirits, told me where to find the backup key,"

Desi says, a shy smile on their face.

I gasp. "You have the gift? Like your nana?"

"Si!" Desi beams. "She said sometimes a big shock, like knowing Mason was trying to kill you, could trigger it." Their eyes cloud over. "I pounded on the door. I could hear Mason yelling, you coughing. I was so frantic—and then the spirits, they spoke to me, they told me to feel under your mailbox for the key."

I nod. "My dad taped it there in case we needed it."

Desi runs their hand through their hair. "I'd just taken it out when Jenna came running up. We burst in together. She was so scared for you, Kate. I know you have your differences, but she loves you."

"Yeah," I say softly. "I saw that. Thank you for saving my life. And hey—I'm so glad you can talk to spirits now! I know it's what you wanted. Maybe we can team up sometime, our gifts helping each other."

"I'd like that." Desi grabs my hand. "We'd be awesome together. We already are."

"And now I don't have to feel guilty asking you to practice with me."

Desi shoves me lightly. "I would've anyway. Anything to get you to have visions without triggering an attack."

"Yeah." I shudder. "I never want to get this close to death again."

Desi clenches my hand, their other hand becoming a fist. "I felt so helpless. So freaking scared."

I cover their hand with mine. "I'm okay now. The police found Mason this morning. And you saved me, Desi. You and Jenna. I'm grateful you came."

"Of course I came!" Desi's eyes fill with tears. "I don't know what I would've done if you hadn't made it."

"But I did make it," I say.

Desi sniffs. "Damned right you did." Their mouth curves up in a trembly smile, and they squeeze my hand, then let go. "Hey, you'll never believe it—Ms. Hirano is making each of us read one of the banned books that you, me, and Imani suggested. Gabby had a fit."

I roll my eyes. "Of course she did."

"I told her she should read something from your list. She looked like she was going to combust!"

I laugh, then cough.

Desi's smile falters.

"I'm okay," I tell them.

Desi crosses their arms. "You'd better be. I need you around. Anyway, I might've gotten a bit emotional. Said you'd almost died from an asthma attack, and that I'd heard some people had been putting you down. I told them they don't want that on their conscience."

Wow. I stare at them.

"After class, Gabby told me to tell you that she's sorry." Desi narrows their eyes at me and waits.

"Yeah." I sigh. "She was the one who was bullying me the most."

"Figures. But I think she's trying to change her jackass behaviour."

"I'll believe it when I see it," I say.

"Fair enough." Desi shifts their weight. "When you get out of here—"

"I get out tomorrow."

"Can I come see you? Maybe we could do something—at your place, if you need to rest. We could read, cuddle, play cards, watch a movie, whatever you want."

"I'd love that," I say. "Come here." I tug their shirt, pulling them down toward me.

Desi leans in and kisses me softly, their hand cupping my cheek.

They feel so right—their lips against mine, their hand on my cheek, them in my life with their fierce sense of justice, their deep empathy, their strong love. And I almost lost them. Almost lost my own life. I never want to risk either again.

Our kiss feels sweeter than before, maybe because I know how lucky I am to be alive. To have Desi truly see me and love me. To have a family who cares, and who's willing to accept something they don't understand.

For the first time in a long time I don't care that my life is so restricted by my asthma, or that I can see things most other people can't. I'm grateful to be alive, to date Desi, to take part in things I enjoy. I'm going to push to do more. And I know that Desi and Nana are right; my visions are a gift. They kept two people alive. Three if I include myself. They helped me right a wrong. And they helped me find the human I love.

I touch Desi's cheek. This is the start of something special; I can feel it. I don't need to see it in a vision to believe it.

Desi pulls back to look at me. "Damn. I'm so glad you're here."

I grab their hand. "Me, too. And Desi? You and me—we're better together. We're amazing."

Desi laughs. "I know that. I was just waiting for you to see it."

Did You Enjoy Visions?

Please let others know. It helps get the word out, and helps me write and publish more books.

It really helps to:

Review it. Write a short review on Amazon, Barnes and Noble, GoodReads, Book Bub, or your favorite social network. This is one of the most important ways to help. Thank you!

Recommend it. Let others know you enjoyed this book—in person, online (TikTok, Instagram, FaceBook, etc.). It makes a difference.

"Like" it on Amazon (the "like" button just underneath the title, next to the rating), and/or rate it on Amazon, Barnes and Noble, GoodReads, and/or StoryGraph.

Request it at your local library.

Follow me on social media.

Sign up for my author newsletter; you get a free short story, and hear about upcoming releases, cover reveals, giveaways, book sales, book recommendations, bits of my author life, and other news. https://www.cherylrainfield.com/newsletter/

If you like an author's books, word-of-mouth recommendations are one of the best ways you can help them. If you let others know about my books, you have my heartfelt thanks and appreciation. And I'd love to hear if you've enjoyed them.

Learn more about Cheryl Rainfield's books at CherylRainfield.com.

If you're a YA book reviewer and want a digital review copy of one of my books, email me at Cheryl@CherylRainfield.com.

Resource Guide

Books Mentioned

In the last few years in the US, books have been mass banned by a small group of organized, vocal, right-wing individuals and groups, including Moms For Liberty which is recognized as a hate group. The books that are being targeted are books by and about queer, trans, Black, brown, and Indigenous, mental health, and survivor voices. Seeing ourselves reflected in books is so important, especially when we're part of a marginalized group or groups. The books below (and so many others by and about marginalized groups) can increase empathy, encourage healing, and help us know we're not alone—and they make a great reading list.

Adler, Dahlia. *Going Bicoastal.* Wednesday Books, 2023. ISBN-13: 978-1250871640

Alexie, Sherman. *The Absolutely True Diary of A Part Time Indian.* Little, Brown Books for Young Readers, 2007. ISBN-13: 978-0316013680

Anderson, Laurie Halse. *Speak.* Farrar, Straus and Giroux, 1999. ISBN-13: 978-0374371524

Callender, Kacen. *Felix Ever After.* Balzer + Bray, 2020. ISBN-13: 978-0062820259

Gino, Alex. *Melissa.* Scholastic, 2022. ISBN-13: 978-1338843408

Hopkins, Ellen. *Crank*. Margaret K. McElderry Books, 2010. ISBN-13: 978-1416995135

Jackson, Tiffany D. *Monday's Not Coming*. Katherine Tegen Books, 2018. ISBN-13: 978-0062422675

Johnson, George M. *All Boys Aren't Blue*. Farrar, Straus and Giroux, 2020. ISBN-13: 978-0374312718

Kobabe, Maia. *Gender Queer*. Oni Press, 2019. ISBN-13: 978-1549304002

Lo, Malinda. *Last Night at the Telegraph Club*. Dutton Books for Young Readers, 2021. ISBN-13: 978-0525555254

Rainfield, Cheryl. *Scars*. Westside Books, 2010. ISBN-13: 978-1934813324

Reynolds, Jason and Ibram X. Kendi. *Stamped*. Little, Brown Books for Young Readers, 2020. ISBN-13: 978-0316453691

Rivera, Gabby. *Juliet Takes A Breath*. Dial Books, 2019. ISBN-13: 978-0593108178

Salvatore, Steven. *Can't Take that Away*. Bloomsbury YA, 2021. ISBN-13: 978-1547605309

Shamim, Sarif. *The Athena Protocol*. HarperTeen, 2019. ISBN-13: 978-0062849618

Symes-Smith, Esme. *Sir Callie And The Champions of Helston*. Labyrinth Road, 2022. ISBN-13: 978-0593485774

Thomas, Aiden. *Cemetery Boys.* Swoon Reads, 2020. ISBN-13: 978-1250250469

Thomas, Angie. *The Hate U Give.* Balzer + Bray, 2018. ISBN-13: 978-0062871350

Domestic Violence

Love Is Respect: National Teen Dating Abuse Hotline
http://www.loveisrespect.org/
1.866.331.9474 Text: LOVEIS to 22522

National Domestic Violence Hotline (USA)
https://www.thehotline.org/
1-800-799-7233

StrongHearts Native Helpline (USA)
https://strongheartshelpline.org/
1-844-7NATIVE (762-8483)

Assaulted Women's Helpline (Canada)
http://www.awhl.org/
Toll Free: 1-866-863-0511

Talk For Healing: Indigenous Women (ON, Canada)
http://www.talk4healing.com/
1-855-554-4325

Refuge: National Domestic Helpline (UK)
https://www.nationaldahelpline.org.uk/
0808 2000 247, 24/7

Domestic Violence Myths and Facts
http://www.hiddenhurt.co.uk/domestic_violence_myths.html

2SLGBTQIA+ Crisis Lines And Suicide Prevention

The Trevor Project (USA) For queer teens
http://www.thetrevorproject.org/
1-866-488-7386 or text TREVOR to 1-202-304-1200

LGBT Youthline (Canada)
https://www.youthline.ca/
647-694-4275

Trans Lifeline
https://translifeline.org/
Canada (877) 330-6366
US (877) 565-8860

It Gets Better Project (USA)
http://www.itgetsbetter.org/

Desi LGBTQ+ Helpline for South Asians (USA)
https://www.deqh.org/
908-367-3374

StrongHearts Native Helpline (USA)
https://strongheartshelpline.org/
1-844-7NATIVE (762-8483)

Blackline for Black, Indigenous, People of Colour through

LGBTQ+ Black femme lens (USA)
  https://gabe-berlin-95fm.squarespace.com/
  1 (800) 604-5841

Sexual Assault, Sexual Abuse, And Incest

RAINN
https://www.rainn.org
Hotline: 800.656.HOPE (4673)

Survivors of Incest Anonymous
https://siawso.org/

1 in 6: Male Survivors of Sexual Assault
https://1in6.org/

HAVOCA : Help for Adult Victims Of Child Abuse
https://www.havoca.org/

Suicide Prevention

National Suicide Prevention Lifeline (US)
http://www.suicidepreventionlifeline.org/

Youth Suicide Prevention (Canada)
http://www.youthsuicide.ca/

Crisis Services Canada
https://www.crisisservicescanada.ca/en/

1-833-456-4566

Befrienders Worldwide: Find a hotline in your country
https://www.befrienders.org/help-and-support

Crisis Textline: Get Support Through Text for anxiety,
depression, self-harm, suicide, gun violence, eating disorders, and
more.
https://www.crisistextline.org/
Text HOME to connect with a crisis counsellor: US and Canada:
text 741741 | UK: text 85258 | Ireland: text 50808.

Asthma

Asthma Attacks: Learn More
http://www.noattacks.org/

Teens Health: Asthma Center
http://kidshealth.org/teen/centers/asthma_center.html

Asthma and Allergy Foundation of America
http://www.aafa.org/index.cfm

About The Author

Photo by Courtney Evers

Cheryl Rainfield (they/she) is a trans nonbinary lesbian author of the award-winning SCARS, a novel about a queer teen sexual abuse survivor who uses self-harm to cope and must save herself; the award-winning HUNTED, a novel about a teen who is a telepath in a world where any paranormal power is illegal; and STAINED, about a teen who is abducted and must rescue herself. Cheryl Rainfield is an incest and cult torture survivor who is an avid reader and writer. Through their work, Cheryl tries to help people know they are not alone, no matter where their pain comes from. They are an advocate for abuse survivors, people who've self-harmed, and the 2SLGBTQIA+ community. They live in Toronto.

Cheryl Rainfield has been said to write with "great empathy and compassion" (VOYA) and to write stories that "can, perhaps, save a life." (CM Magazine) School Library Journal said of their work: "[readers] will be on the edge of their seats."

Their book SCARS has repeatedly been banned by far-right conservatives in a mass book-ban movement led by hate groups such as Moms For Liberty.

They invite you to sign up for their newsletter on CherylRainfield.com, where you can get a free 45-page SCARS short story, news about their latest books, bookish tidbits, and more.

You Can Find Cheryl On:

Their website CherylRainfield.com

TikTok for book recommendations, honest talk about cult torture, healing from trauma, mental health, book banning, being queer in a homophobic world, & more:
https://www.tiktok.com/@cherylrainfield

Facebook:
https://www.facebook.com/cheryl.rainfield

Instagram:
https://www.instagram.com/cherylrainfield/

Twitter:
https://twitter.com/CherylRainfield

YouTube:
https://www.youtube.com/@Cheryl.Rainfield

BookBub for book recommendations:
https://www.bookbub.com/profile/cheryl-rainfield

Pinterest:
http://pinterest.com/cherylrainfield/

BlueSky:
https://bsky.app/profile/cherylrainfield.bsky.social

Acknowledgements

My deep and heartfelt thanks to:

Jean, whose love, support, and encouragement nurtures my soul, and who is like a mother to me. Your compassion, encouragement, and love are a balm to my soul.

Evelyn Fazio, my dear friend and chosen family, who was the first editor to believe in me, buying and editing Scars and Hunted, and who has continued to believe in me, encourage me, and love me, talking with me most every day.

Julie Schoerke, my dear friend and chosen family who was my wonderful book publicist, helping me get my books out there, and who believes in me, cares about me, and encourages me.

My dear friend Hilary Cameron, her partner Emmet, their kids Tobin and Kella, who have been cheerleading me along my edits, all the ups and downs of the publishing industry, every ban of my books, and who accept and love me as me; they are part of my chosen family and I love them.

Leanne, Karen, Laura, Joey, and Matilda and their parents Ivette and Kamil, who also believe in me and love me and are part of my chosen family, and who I love back.

Gail Fisher-Taylor, who gave me my first real safety and support I ever had, and who believed my trauma memories.

Authors Nelsa Roberto, Erin Thomas, and Karen Krossing who

read previous versions of this book and gave me valuable feedback.

Paul Coccia, award-winning author of books *I Got You Babe*, *The Player*, *Cub*, and more great queer YA books, who generously read and blurbed Visions, even though he was swamped with work.

Joanne Levy, award-winning author of *Bird Brain*, *Sorry For Your Loss*, *The Book of Elsie*, and more moving MG books, for kindly and generously swooping in to help me last minute with formatting issues I was having with MS Word.

The wonderful community of fellow children's and YA writers.

All the many readers and book lovers who've written to tell me how much SCARS, HUNTED, and STAINED touched you, and who wrote reviews. Your emails, messages, and comments full of love for my books feed my soul.

And especially the readers who've stayed in touch over the years, always wanted more of my books, and continued to tell me what a difference my books and I made for you. I'm grateful for you all.

Your Free eBook Is Waiting

Kendra's father's trial is only three months away, and she's dreading it. Her mother has become critical, and keeps fighting with Kendra's girlfriend Meghan.

Kendra hasn't cut in months, but everything is starting to feel too hard. Will she be able to keep from cutting?

Grab a copy FADED SCARS, a 38-page SCARS short story
https://www.cherylrainfield.com/newsletter/

Other Titles By Cheryl Rainfield

Award-winning SCARS

"Scars is a brave novel, a read-in-one-sitting-except-when-you-have-to-put-it-down-to-breathe novel."
- Ellen Hopkins, author of Burned, a National Book Award nominee and an ALA Best Book for Young Adults.

Kendra must face her past and stop hurting herself—before it's too late....
An edgy, realistic, and hopeful novel about a teen survivor of sexual abuse who uses self-harm to cope.

SCARS is a Governor General Literary Award finalist, #1 in ALA's 2011 Top 10 Quick Picks for Reluctant Readers, and is on ALA's Rainbow List (LGBTQIA+ recommended books). SCARS received a starred review from School Library Journal. The arms on the cover are the author's.

"Scars is the 'must' read for any teen. I couldn't put it down."
- Gail Giles, author of Right Behind You, a 2009 ALA Quick Pick for Reluctant Young Adult Readers

Though it is currently out of print you can still buy it new as an audiobook (Libro.fm, Audible US, Audible CAN, etc.), find it used in print, or borrow it from your library.

Award-winning HUNTED

"Spellbound by this one! HUNTED's got my vote for the sharpest, most thought-provoking fantasy I've read in a long time. It's hard not to fall in love with resilient, defiant Caitlyn, whose voice is as tough as it is pure."
- Adele Griffin, Author of Where I Want to Be, National Book Award finalist, Kirkus Best Book, ALA Best Book

Caitlyn is a telepath in a world where having any paranormal power is illegal. She's on the run from government ParaTroopers. When Caitlyn falls for Alex, a Normal, and discovers dangerous renegade paranormals, she must choose between staying in hiding to protect herself, or taking a stand to save the world.

Finalist for the Monica Hughes Award for Science Fiction & Fantasy. "This is a marvelous read for those teens who loved The Hunger Games." - VOYA

Award-winning STAINED

"Powerful. I raced through it, wanting to know if Sarah would find a way to escape both her captor and her self-doubts. A real nail-biter!"
—April Henry, NYT-bestselling author of The Girl Who Was Supposed to Die

Sarah, a teen with a port-wine stain, is abducted and must find a way to rescue herself.

"A compelling, gutting, and ultimately triumphant read. You won't want to stop turning pages — Or blink. Or breathe. — until you reach the very last one."
—Jennifer Brown, award-winning author of Hate List

Bank Street College Center for Children's Literature's Best Books of The Year ages Fourteen and Up (2014), and an ALAN Pick for August 2013.

Two hi-lo (high interest, low vocabulary) books for teens:

Dragon Speaker: The Last Dragon (HIP Books, 2009)

A boy is the only one who can hear—and save—the last dragon.

SkinWalkers: Walking Both Sides (HIP Books, 2011)

A girl, half-human and half-shapeshifter, must find a way to bring both worlds together.